Winter Weepies

Also in the Point Romance series:
Look out for:

The Love Collection
Various

Cover Girl 1: Assignment in Spain
Lorna Read

Can't Buy Me Love
Nigel Robinson

Point Romance

Winter Weepies

edited by
J. Moffatt

SCHOLASTIC

Scholastic Children's Books
Commonwealth House, 1–19 New Oxford Street,
London WC1A 1NU, UK
a division of Scholastic Ltd
London ~ New York ~ Toronto ~ Sydney ~ Auckland

First published by Scholastic Ltd, 1996

This anthology copyright © Scholastic Ltd, 1996

ISBN 0 590 13750 6

Typeset by TW Typesetting, Midsomer Norton, Avon
Printed by Cox & Wyman Ltd, Reading, Berks.

Acknowledgements

All of the stories are original and appear for the first time in this volume.

The following are the copyright owners of the stories:

The Cinderella Syndrome copyright © 1996 Sue Welford

Outsider copyright © 1996 Jill Eckersley

Love by e-mail copyright © 1996 Amber Vane

Too Far To Go copyright © 1996 Alison Creaghan

The Snow Queen copyright © 1996 Robyn Turner

Island Return copyright © 1996 Sally James

Magic Carpet copyright © 1996 Lorna Read

An Unhappy Christmas and a Happy New Year
  copyright © 1996 Bette Paul

Out in the Cold copyright © 1996 Helen McCann

Contents

The Cinderella Syndrome

Sue Welford

It was bleak mid-winter. Frosty winds were making moan and it was Sarah's wedding day.

Vicky knew it was going to snow. She could see the sky through the gap in her curtains. Grey, leaden. It matched her mood perfectly.

Vicky gazed at the photo of Sarah and herself on the dressing table. Twins. Sarah, tall, blonde, gorgeous, scatty. Vicky, not so tall, not so fair, glasses, sensible.

"Oh, you're not at all alike, are you?" people used to say when they were introduced. What they really meant was how could ordinary old Vicky possibly be the twin of the beautiful creature that was her sister?

The bedroom door opened and Sarah came bouncing through. She thrust back the corner of the duvet and got into bed.

"Budge up." She lay down, shivering. "It's

going to snow," she said, snuggling close. She gazed up at the ceiling. "Perfect," she said. "Just what I wanted."

Only Sarah would want snow on her wedding day. Most people wanted warmth and sunshine. Not Sarah. The snow would make a perfect backdrop for her dream dress of pale rose-coloured wild silk, her bright sheaf of scarlet roses and green ribbon.

Snow would make a wonderful setting too for Sarah's bridesmaids' dresses. Vicky's was hanging on the wardrobe door. She could hardly bear to look. Red velvet with a white fake-fur trim. Fake-fur muff to match. Sarah couldn't have chosen anything worse if she tried. The thought of waltzing down the aisle stuffed into a scarlet velvet dress with black button boots was almost a fate worse than death.

Mum had seen her face when she tried it on for the first time.

"It looks lovely, Vicky," she said, standing beside her in front of the mirror. "Honestly."

Vicky had pulled a face. "Come off it, Mum, it looks gross."

But Mum had insisted. "It's just not the kind of thing you normally wear, that's all," she said.

Vicky had laughed. "It's not the kind of thing anyone *normally* wears."

Mum had laughed too. "It's Sarah's day," she said. "Don't spoil it for her."

Vicky had turned to her mother in horror. "You know I wouldn't do that!"

"I know." Mum had hugged her and they had laughed a bit more … and cried. They both felt emotional about Sarah's wedding. Vicky more than she realized.

Mum had held her at arm's length. "You're not unhappy about the wedding, are you, Vicky? I know it will seem strange for you, Sarah being married."

"No, of course I'm not." Vicky said, not at all convinced she was telling the absolute truth. "If Sarah's happy, then I'm happy, you know that."

"That's good, then," Mum had said.

So Vicky had kept quiet about the dress. She meant what she said. She wouldn't have spoiled things for Sarah for all the world.

One thing Vicky was grateful for. None of her college friends were going to be there to see her in it. Thank God. All the old aunts, distant cousins and grandparents were bad enough. To say nothing of Brian's lot. Even his best mate was coming over from Australia. It was going to be hell. Why Sarah and Brian couldn't just live together like most other couples, Vicky really didn't know.

Sarah was still cuddled up to her in bed. She sighed dramatically.

"I wonder what Brian's up to?"

"Probably got a vile hangover," Vicky said.

"He'd better not." Sarah wriggled closer, warmer now. Vicky could smell her perfume from last night. They'd been out to a club with some old school friends. Danced until one when Dad insisted on coming to pick them up. "I'll kill him if he has," Sarah was saying. "Luke promised he'd look after him."

"Luke?"

"His friend from Oz, remember?"

"Oh ... yes."

Luke had only arrived a couple of days before. Sarah hadn't met him yet. Only spoken to him on the phone.

"I hope he'll be OK as best man," Sarah was saying. "Not being here for the rehearsal and everything."

"I'm sure he'll be fine." Vicky didn't really know why she said that. She didn't know anything about Brian's mate from Australia. He could be a crazy drop-out for all she knew. All she did know was that he and Brian had been best friends for years. They had been at school together until Luke and his family emigrated a few years ago.

Sarah was clutching her hands together and sighing. "Oh Vic, just think, in five hours' time I'll be Mrs Brian Jenkins."

"Ugh," Vicky said.

Sarah laughed and thumped her on the shoulder. "Don't be so horrible."

Vicky chuckled. "I'm not. If you want to spend your life in domestic bliss, it's up to you."

Vicky's heart turned over when she thought about Sarah being Mrs Brian Jenkins. She got a strange feeling right in the pit of her stomach. She didn't really know why. It wasn't jealousy. Strangely, she had never been jealous of her sister. A little envious sometimes. Nothing more. Maybe she felt a pang of regret then? It wasn't that she still loved Brian. She had got over him long ago. But still, deep down, there was the thought that it might have been *her* walking up the aisle today. And it could have been Sarah who was stuffed into that vile red dress. Although, of course, if it had been, *she* would have looked wonderful. As if she'd just stepped off the catwalk.

Vicky had known it would be a mistake. Introducing Brian to Sarah. Bringing him home from college for the weekend. She remembered his face when he first saw her twin sister.

They had been sitting in the front room watching TV. Mum had gone off into the kitchen dithering about with eggs and cheese and stuff for that night's supper. Vicky had thought Sarah was away for the weekend. But she had turned up, bright as mid summer's day, a couple of hours after they got there.

"Vic!" Sarah had come through the door like the whirlwind that she was. She had thrown her arms round her sister. "You look great."

"Liar." Vicky had hugged and kissed her like they always did. Over Sarah's shoulder she saw Brian. His mouth was open. He had that kind of glazed look in his eye. She'd seen it a million times before when guys met Sarah for the first time.

"Brian..." Vicky had disentangled herself from Sarah's arms. "This is Sarah," she had said needlessly. After all, who else could it have been?

"Hi, Brian." Sarah had held out her hand. "Great to meet you at last."

"At last," Vicky had giggled. "We've only known each other three months."

Brian had got up from the settee in a kind of daze.

"Th ... thought you were going to be away." He gazed at Sarah like Dracula gazes at a throbbing artery. Vicky could almost see his mouth watering. His Adam's apple was going up and down like a Yo-Yo.

Sarah beamed him one of her irresistible smiles. She didn't mean to do it. It was just the way she greeted everyone.

"Thought I'd better give you the once-over," she said. "I don't want my sister going out with anyone undesirable."

Brian had laughed and stammered and laughed again. Vicky's heart had sunk down to the soles of her Doc Martens. Brian never stammered. He had more self-confidence than most of the blokes she knew. Vicky realized he was hooked. She'd lost him from that very first moment. She should have been used to it. Sarah had pinched her boyfriends before. It wasn't that she did it on purpose. Blokes could just not resist those baby blue eyes. But Vicky found herself *really* minding this time. She'd been crazy about Brian ever since she first saw him in the pub. And he'd been crazy about her. At least until he saw Sarah.

Vicky hadn't been able to bring herself to speak to Sarah for weeks even though she knew it was tearing their parents to pieces.

Eventually, Vicky decided it just wasn't worth it. Brian loved Sarah and Sarah loved Brian. There was nothing in the world she could do about it. So, for Mum and Dad's sake, she pretended she'd got over it. In reality though, she had hated her sister. A secret, smouldering hate that threatened to ruin their relationship for ever.

The hatred had gone away eventually. Just as it always had whenever they had fallen out over something.

Or had it? Now, thinking about him, his easy smile, his brown eyes ... the way his black hair looked tousled first thing in the morning... All of a sudden, Vicky wasn't absolutely sure. She'd had boyfriends since but, she had to admit, none had matched up to Brian.

Sarah was gazing at her. A slight frown creased her perfect eyebrows.

"You are looking forward to today, aren't you, Sist?" Sarah had always called Vicky that. Vicky said it sounded like some kind of growth but Sarah had only laughed.

"Course I am," Vicky said quickly. "It's going to be absolutely wonderful." She really wasn't sure if she was fibbing or not.

"And you forgive me?"

"Forgive you?" Vicky pretended she didn't know what Sarah was on about.

"For pinching Brian?"

Vicky sighed. "Come off it, Sar, we've been through all that ages ago."

"I know." Sarah was still gazing at her intently. She had a way of looking at you that made you think she could see right into your mind. "But I still feel guilty ... even now."

Vicky hugged her. "Don't," she said. "It's all over and forgotten. Water under the bridge."

Sarah hugged her back and Vicky could hear tears in her voice. "I'm really glad," Sarah said.

The door opened and Mum came in carrying a tray aloft like a head waiter.

"Breakfast for the bride and bridesmaid," she said gaily. "Sit up you two."

The whirlwind, fairytale day had begun.

First came the beautician complete with mobile couch and white coat. Leg wax, facial, make-up, the full works. Vicky really didn't see why she had to suffer the agony of having her legs stripped but Sarah insisted.

"My treat," she said.

Then the hairdresser turned up. She cooed over Sarah's shining tresses: sighed over Vicky's frizzy mop.

"A good job you're not wearing a head-dress," she'd said. "We'd never get one on over this lot."

Vicky didn't say that was one thing she had refused point blank. The dress she could just about handle. Flowers in her hair, or worse, a fake-fur headband … never.

When they had finished, Vicky had to admit they'd done a good job. On her as well as Sarah.

"I'm so pleased you've got contact lenses now," Sarah said. Vicky didn't let on she still mostly wore her glasses. It had been one of the major fears of Sarah's life that one day she would have to wear them too.

"If one falls out in church then it'll be your fault for nagging me into getting them," Vicky said. She could just see herself crawling about on hands and knees in that revolting dress looking for her contact lens.

Sarah giggled. She sounded suddenly nervous. As if she had only just realized the gigantic step she was about to take.

She was gazing down at her newly-painted scarlet fingernails. "Ooh, Sist..." she wailed. "It's almost time."

Then there was lunch, which Sarah couldn't eat. Vicky ate enough for both of them. It was such a treat to have Mum's home cooking she was damned if she would let it go to waste.

Then there was the putting on of the wedding dress. Vicky could hear giggles coming from Mum and Dad's room. Sarah was in there with Mum. Vicky was in the other room, wriggling into her bridesmaid's outfit. Their cousin Gill had got hers on already. Gill looked great in her dress. Vicky, taller, slender too, but bigger boned than Gill, decided she looked like Mother Christmas. All she needed was a sack of goodies and a couple of reindeer and the picture would be complete.

She was still staring at herself in the mirror when Mum called from the other room.

"Come and see, you two. Come and see the bride!"

Dad was in there too now. He had tears in his eyes. He put an arm round them both.

"My girls," he said with a little shake in his voice. "My beautiful girls."

Vicky suddenly wanted to cry. Sarah was looking at her. "Don't you dare," she warned in a trembly voice. "I don't want a chief bridesmaid with mascara all down her cheeks."

It was freezing in the church. So cold Vicky thought she would have a constant drip at the end of her nose. She could hardly see Brian. Just the back of his head. Part of that was obscured by the gigantic meringue Sarah wore over her face. It was quite the fluffiest veil Vicky had ever come across. Sarah never did do things by halves. Vicky had thought Brian would look daft in his wedding gear. The ghastly jacket. The stupid top hat. But even though she could only see half of him she knew with a sinking heart that when he turned round he was going to look absolutely fantastic. His profile as he looked down at Sarah was soft with adoration.

Vicky swallowed. She wished she was somewhere else. At college, on a beach somewhere ... the moon. Anywhere but here. She hadn't quite realized what effect seeing Brian would have on her. She must be going mad. She was over him, *really* over him, yet here she was at her sister's wedding feeling unaccountably close to crying her eyes out.

Vicky shifted uncomfortably. The revolting frock itched like mad. She leaned sideways. She could see the best man better than she could see Brian. He was staring up at the stained-glass window. Tall. Tanned face, sun-bleached blond hair curling at the neck. He shrugged his shoulders around, uncomfortable in his starchy wedding suit. Vicky bet he wished he was surfing some fabulous Ozzie beach. She knew exactly how he felt.

Brian was saying his vows. His deep, clear voice rang out round the church. His mum was weeping quietly into a lace-edged hanky. Its perfume wafted across to Vicky and almost made her sneeze. She held her fake-fur muff up to her nose. Sarah would never forgive her if she sneezed while Brian was making his pledge.

"From this day forward ... till death us do part..."

Then, suddenly, it was all over. The bells were ringing. Everyone was smiling, mopping away tears. Sarah had thrown back her meringue and they were turning round. Vicky swallowed. She'd been right. Brian looked amazing. He smiled at her as she handed Sarah her flowers. Her brain did a blip and they were back in her room at college. Lying on the bed. Vicky was reading him a poem.

He was gazing up at her as she read. She smiled at him over the top of her glasses. Her heart had been full of love for him. She had no doubt about it. It was the real thing at last.

Brian had stroked her hair softly and smiled back. The same smile he was smiling at her now. The whole world seemed to dissolve as she stared into his eyes. Everyone ... Sarah, Mum and Dad, Gill, Luke ... none of them were really there. They were all just figments of her imagination. There was just Vicky and Brian for that one, brief moment in time.

She wanted to reach out to him, touch his hair ... his face.

Brian winked at her. An affectionate, *brotherly* wink. He turned away, gliding down the aisle with his bride on his arm.

The spell was broken.

Vicky wiped a tear away and hoped he hadn't seen. To hell with smudged mascara.

"Hi! Don't tell me. You're Sarah's twin. Aren't we supposed to walk down the aisle together or something?"

Vicky came to. "Er ... sorry?"

"You're the chief bridesmaid," the best man was saying. "We're supposed to walk out of the church together, yeah?"

"Oh..." Vicky mumbled. "Er ... yes."

He was staring at her. She could see by his expression he thought she looked awful. His startling blue eyes were taking in her face, her hair, the long swathe of red velvet, the stupid muff hanging round her neck. It was a wonder he didn't fall over laughing.

"Hey." He was still staring. He probably couldn't believe what he was seeing. "Cheer up. This is your sister's wedding day."

Vicky wondered if Brian had told Luke that he had once been her boyfriend. That Sarah had taken away his heart.

She swallowed and managed a grin. "Yes, sorry."

Whatever happened, Sarah mustn't know how she was feeling. If a complete stranger had noticed, then she'd be bound to.

She walked beside him down the aisle.

"Are you upset she's got married?" He sounded like someone out of *Neighbours*.

"Er ... no, of course not. I'm happy for her."

"You'll miss her though, won't you? Being twins and all." He almost tripped over, staring at her instead of where he was going.

She wished he'd shut up. Was she going to be lumbered with him for the rest of the day?

"Er ... yes," she said, still not looking at him. "I'm away at college though, so we're used to being apart."

"It won't be the same though, will it?"

She glanced at him and realized he was right. It wouldn't be the same. Not ever.

He had put on his top hat. It looked so ridiculous over his long blond hair she almost burst out laughing. In fact, she reckoned they made a good pair. Like something out of *The Munsters*.

"No," she said softly. "It won't."

Mum had threaded in behind, arm in arm with Brian's dad. Then Dad, escorting Brian's mum as if she was the Queen.

It had been snowing when they arrived but now it had stopped. The sky had cleared and the sun had come out. Everything shone and glittered with a million snow diamonds.

Vicky moved away from the bridal pair. She stood, ankle deep in snow, watching the photographer ordering everyone around. She put her hands inside her ridiculous muff, glad suddenly of the warmth.

There was a movement beside her. It was Luke, staring. "Beautiful," he said.

"Yes," she answered. "Isn't it? Sarah wanted it to snow on her wedding day."

He stamped his feet up and down and hugged himself for warmth. "Bloody cold, though."

She couldn't help grinning. "It usually is when it snows."

"Too right." He grinned back.

Her sister's wish had come true. Providing no one died of exposure while the photos were being taken, then everything *was* perfect.

No one did die of exposure. One or two of

the elderly aunts looked close to it though. There was an intangible sigh of relief when the photographer had finished.

Vicky felt herself close to tears again when the horse and carriage arrived to take the bride and groom to the reception.

Brian did the right thing as usual. He picked up his bride and carried her along the snowy church path to the waiting carriage. Everyone clapped. Vicky sighed. It seemed Brian just could not put a foot wrong!

They looked wonderful. Sarah and Brian ... man and wife. They waved as the horse trotted off along the snowy road. It was like something out of a Hollywood movie.

Vicky sighed again. She watched until they were out of sight.

"Come on," Mum said, sniffing. She put her arm across Vicky's shoulders. "Let's go."

"Want a lift?" Luke was there, jangling Brian's car keys in his tanned fingers. "I'm supposed to look after the bridesmaids, aren't I?" He seemed pretty anxious to do the right thing.

When Vicky looked, Gill was already in the front seat. She was looking at herself in the vanity mirror, patting her smooth hair.

"It's OK, thanks," Vicky said. "I'll go with Mum and Dad."

"Yeah? You sure?" He ran his hands through his thick hair. He seemed to have ditched the hat somewhere. He really wasn't bad looking if you liked the rugged, outdoor type.

"Honestly," Vicky said.

"See you later, then."

The reception was at the poshest hotel in the area. It had once been a stately home. The grand ballroom was alive with candelabra glow as the guests arrived in the gloom of the fading winter afternoon.

Afterwards, Vicky could hardly remember the meal, the speeches, the toasts, the cake. It wasn't that she'd had too much champagne. It just all seemed so unreal. Like watching a play. What she *did* remember was staring at Luke as he made his speech. How everyone laughed at his tales of the things he and Brian had got up to as kids. The same old stuff about how lucky Brian was. How, if he didn't live down-under, then he might have been the one to sweep Sarah off her feet. Vicky felt sure he meant it too. Sarah looked stunningly beautiful on this, the happiest day of her life. She needn't have worried. As a best man, Luke was a definite hit.

Later, after Vicky had done the rounds of all the relatives, old and new, she desperately needed a breath of fresh air. The band were just setting up for their first number as she made her way towards the door.

She felt a hand on her arm. She turned. Luke. He had changed out of his wedding outfit into a pair of jeans, a white shirt under a black biker's jacket. Maybe it was the champagne but he suddenly looked devastatingly handsome. His eyes were even more amazingly blue in the light from the lamps: his shoulders broad under the jacket. Vicky blinked and swallowed. Was she going crazy? She liked the dark, brooding, sensitive type of guy, not the rugged, outdoor type. She *must* have had too much to drink.

He had obviously seen the surprise on her face.

"Couldn't stand looking like a penguin any longer," he explained, looking down at himself. "Think they'll chuck me out?"

Vicky shook her head. "Shouldn't think

so," she said. She plucked at the hideous velvet of her skirt. "I'd give anything to get out of this."

"Too hot, is it?"

"No," she smiled. "Too ghastly."

"Want to dance? We're supposed to, aren't we?"

If he was asking her to dance because he was *supposed* to then Vicky didn't want to know.

"It's OK, thanks," she said. "I'm just going to get some fresh air. Dance with Gill, you're *supposed* to be looking after her too, you know."

She didn't mean to say it so sharply. It just came out like that. It was bad enough going around looking like a Christmas cracker without anyone feeling they were obliged to dance with you.

Sarah and Brian were the only ones on the floor. They looked perfect swaying to the strains of some romantic ballad. Brian bent his head to kiss his bride, Vicky looked away.

Luke raised his blond eyebrows and shrugged. "OK," he said and walked off in Gill's direction.

Vicky went through the big double doors and out on to the terrace. It was a beautiful evening. The sky was a dome of stars. The snow glittered in the moonlight. Every blade of grass, every branch twinkled with a million diamonds. It was so beautiful it took her breath away. She brushed the snow from one of the stone terrace seats and sat down. Through the glass of the doors she could see the dance floor was crowded. People whirling, dancing, laughing. She could see Luke bobbing around with Gill. Her face was raised to his. They were laughing about something. Everyone was having a great time. Everyone but her. She had been smiling all afternoon, putting on a brave face. But deep in her heart was a sadness she couldn't begin to explain.

She was just beginning to feel cold when the door opened and a figure slipped out. Luke. It looked as if he was still taking his job as best man seriously.

"You'll freeze to death out here." He sat down beside her.

"You really don't have to look after me," she said. "I'm perfectly OK."

"Yeah?" He leaned forward, elbows on his knees. "What a beautiful night."

"Yes." To Vicky's horror her voice cracked up. She burst into tears.

"Hey…"

She felt Luke's arm go round her, pull her close. She turned her head and sobbed into the cold leather of his coat.

"I'm sorry," she croaked. She tried to regain control but couldn't. She felt a twit. "I'm really sorry."

He let her cry for a while. Then he took a spotless white hanky from his pocket.

"Here, blow your nose and tell me what's wrong."

She blew her nose loudly and wiped the smudged mascara from her cheeks. She must look more of a sight than ever. Thank God there was only the moonlight to see by.

She shook her head and tried to clear her throat. "I don't know what's wrong, that's the trouble."

At least he wasn't looking at her. He was just holding her close, staring out over the frosted garden as if he couldn't take his eyes off it.

"I reckon it's Brian," he said.

She shook her head. "Brian? Yes, no … I don't know."

"I thought as much. I saw the way you looked at him."

"Did you know … about me and Brian, I

mean?" She was getting her voice back now. Speaking as if she was Vicky again and not some croaking red velvet witch.

"Yeah, he told me you'd had a thing going once," Luke confessed.

Vicky began to shiver. Hypothermia loomed.

Luke dragged his eyes away from the scenery. He shrugged off his jacket and put it round her shoulders. She tried to protest.

"No, you'll freeze." She thought of the Ozzie midsummer sun he must have left behind.

"It's OK," he insisted. "I'll let you know before I'm about to keel over." He looked at her. "I'm really sorry," he said. "About Brian, I mean. I guess you're finding it hard to come to terms with."

For some stupid reason Vicky was surprised a hunky guy like him could be so understanding. Even if what he said was true. Which it wasn't. Not really.

She fiddled with the gold chain round her neck. Sarah had given it to her for their eighteenth birthday. She had given Sarah one too. The same, although they hadn't planned it. That kind of thing often happened. As if they were able to read each other's thoughts.

Sarah...

Vicky suddenly realized what had been the matter with her all along. It was Sarah she was mourning for. Mourning because things could never be the same between them again. But that was life. Everything, every*one* changes. Things couldn't possibly stay the same for ever.

Vicky gazed at Luke. He was wrong about Brian. Totally wrong. She'd realized some time ago that she really couldn't care less about him. She couldn't pinpoint the exact moment. Maybe it was when he'd carried Sarah across the snow? It had been *just* the right thing to do. That's what was wrong with Brian. He was too perfect. Everyone had to have *some* faults otherwise they weren't real.

Luke was staring back at her. She seemed to be suddenly drowning in the ocean blueness of his eyes.

"Yes," she murmured although she didn't know why. What she should really have said was "no". She should tell Luke he was wrong. Tell him she couldn't care less about Brian any more. But her voice was cracking up again and she found she couldn't correct herself. All she managed was a wan smile.

She suddenly realized Luke was twisting a lock of her hair gently round his fingers. His eyes seemed to be burning holes in her face.

"You know you look really beautiful in that dress," he said.

Vicky's jaw dropped. "Beautiful?" She plucked at the hated material again. "I think it's ghastly."

"No," he said. He lifted a lock of her hair, gazing at it as if he'd found gold at the end of the rainbow. "It brings out the colour of your eyes. The highlights in your hair. Didn't anyone tell you?"

They had, of course, but she hadn't believed them.

She shook her head wordlessly.

Not surprisingly, he assumed that meant *no*.

"I guess everyone only had eyes for the bride," he said softly. "Except me."

Suddenly Vicky wasn't a bit cold any more. In fact, she felt quite hot. Her heart was thudding, her palms beginning to feel moist. She didn't want to think about Brian ever again. She didn't even want to think about Sarah. All she could think about was Luke... Luke bending his head towards her, touching her lips softly with his...

"Hey, you two, they're going. Come and see them off." Dad stood in the doorway. "Come *on*," he urged. "Sarah's been looking for you everywhere."

Luke jumped up and took her hand. "Maybe we could finish this later," he said softly.

"Yes, OK," she whispered. She swayed against him. Maybe she *had* had too much champers after all?

Then they were both caught up in the whirlpool of the departing bride and groom. As soon as she got back in Mum grabbed her arm and hauled her upstairs.

In the room, Sarah's dress lay on the bed, a tumble of wild silk. Sarah had already changed into her going-away outfit. The taxi was at the hotel door waiting to take them to the airport.

Sarah was in the bathroom. When she came out, she threw her arms round Vicky.

"I don't want to go," she wailed.

Vicky hugged her then held her at arm's length. "OK, I'll go instead. I fancy a fortnight in the Caribbean."

Sarah grinned and wiped her eyes. "You'll be lucky." Then she hugged her again. "I'll miss you, Sist."

"Yes," Vicky said. "Me too."

They walked down the stairs, their arms round one another. Everyone was waiting at the bottom. Brian stood there, gooey-eyed. He was holding Sarah's roses.

Sarah took them from him. She thrust them at Vicky.

Vicky stepped back. She had been looking round for Luke but he was nowhere to be seen. "No," she said hastily. "You're supposed to throw them over your shoulder."

But Sarah insisted. "I want you to have them," she said. "No one else."

Then everyone was hugging and kissing, going mad with confetti. They all yelled goodbye, good luck, as Sarah and Brian got into the taxi. Vicky stood to one side, watching as the red tail-lights disappeared down the drive and out into the wide, white world of wedded bliss.

Everyone was going back inside. Vicky found her mum. "Have you seen Luke?"

"Oh, yes, he's taken Aunt Grace home. She wasn't feeling too good."

"Oh." Vicky's heart sank. Luke. Gone. The only person in the world who'd managed to convince her she looked good in red velvet. She heaved a deep sigh. Oh well, no doubt he'd be off back to Australia soon, so what was the use? She would never see him again.

Everyone had gone before Vicky realized she'd still got his jacket. Mum and Dad were saying goodbye to the hotel's manager, thanking him for organizing the wedding reception of the century. There was nothing she could do. She didn't have a clue where he was staying. She would have to send it on to Brian's house and hope that they would be able to get it to him before he went home.

Next morning Vicky felt groggy: an emotional hangover. She lay looking through the gap in the curtains. It was snowing again. Huge, cotton wool flakes fluttering past the window. Yesterday seemed unreal. The ceremony, the reception, out on the terrace with Luke. It was like a fantasy. His jacket, draped over the back of the chair, Sarah's dream dress hanging on the wardrobe door, the red velvet thing hanging beside it. She sighed. It hadn't been a fantasy at all.

Vicky groaned and turned over. No dream, just a fairy tale. Or had it been a pantomime? Had she been a victim of the Cinderella syndrome? She had worn a gorgeous dress, well, it had *become* gorgeous after Luke admired it. She had been to the ball. She had met her prince. But he had gone, her dress hadn't even had a chance to turn into rags and it had been her sister who had got to ride in the carriage.

Vicky buried her face in the pillow. She saw again those blue eyes, smelt the tang of aftershave... She tried to imagine what might have happened if her dad hadn't barged in. She groaned. She had lost again. Sarah 1... Vicky nil... She might as well curl up and die.

Eventually she dragged herself out of bed. She showered and shampooed the lacquer out of her hair. She put on her usual leggings and sloppy sweater. Frizz-dried her hair and tied it up on top of her head. At least she looked normal again.

She took Luke's jacket downstairs and put it on the chair in the hall. She looked up Brian's parents' number and dialled. His mum answered.

"Luke? Oh, yes, he's staying at the hotel where we had the reception."

Vicky's heart soared. "Oh, thanks."

"Wasn't the wedding lovely?" Mrs Jenkins

began. "Didn't your sister look wonderful? And the food…!" She obviously wanted to go over the whole thing again, blow for blow.

Vicky answered as politely as she could. When at last they said goodbye she put the phone down then quickly looked up the hotel's number. Heart thudding, she dialled. She stood tapping her fingers impatiently on the hall table. *Please let him be there,* she said silently. *Please…*

"I'm sorry," the receptionist said after a pause. "He checked out this morning."

So, heart heavy with disappointment, she phoned Brian's mum again.

"He's gone," she said, trying not to sound as if she was about to burst out crying. "Do you have his home address?"

She would just have to pack up the jacket and send it to Oz.

The answer was, no. "Brian's got it, of course," Mrs Jenkins said.

"OK, thanks," Vicky said. "I'll just have to wait till they get back."

She put the phone down with a sigh. She'd been right last night. She really would never see him again.

Vicky went through into the kitchen. *Dad's taken me shopping* a note said on the table. Only Vicky's mum would need to go to Tesco's the day after her daughter's wedding.

Vicky made herself some toast and wandered through into the lounge. She switched on the TV. *The Waltons* was on. She and Sarah had always loved *The Waltons*. Watching it now brought it all back. The fun she and Sarah had had as kids, the way they had always been there for each other, the way they had never been lonely.

Vicky took a bite of toast to try to stop herself from crying. It didn't work. A tear ran down her cheek and on to her plate. The toast tasted horrible, like cardboard. She took out her hanky and blew her nose.

When the programme had finished Vicky went back out into the kitchen with her dirty plate. She put it into the dishwasher. On the worktop stood the remains of the wedding cake. She was just pinching a bit of marzipan when the bell rang.

"Oh God, who's that?" Vicky said to herself. Being sociable was the last thing she felt like.

The bell rang again.

Reluctantly she went to answer it.

A blast of mid-winter air blew in as she opened the door. Luke stood there shivering.

"You ran off with my jacket." He was grinning broadly. He hugged himself and stamped his feet up and down.

"*You* ran off before I could give it back to you." She knew she couldn't possibly hide the joy on her face so what was the point in trying?

She smiled, pulling him inside. Suddenly she felt a million dollars.

He stood in the hall, broad shoulders hunched. He rubbed his hands up and down his arms. There was snow on his head, his shoulders. A flake was melting on his nose. She wanted to hug him, warm him.

He was still grinning and looking at her.

"You don't mind me coming round?" he asked uncertainly.

"Mind? Anyone who thought I looked good in that dress is welcome here any time."

He laughed. "You looked beautiful ... still do."

"Thanks." She lowered her gaze, suddenly serious. "I thought I'd never see you again." She was trying to calm the wild beating of her heart. Surely Cinderella never felt like this?

"Hard luck." He was still stuck in grinning mode. "Here I am."

"I phoned the hotel." Vicky swallowed, trying to sound normal instead of like a girl whose fantasies had just come true. "But you'd already checked out."

"Yep. I didn't even have breakfast. I wanted to catch you…"

She took hold of his hands. "I'm not going anywhere." She tried to pull him into the kitchen where it was warmer.

He held on to her, his broad, tanned fingers encircling hers. She couldn't move. Happiness had rooted her to the spot.

"Neither am I." He had stopped shivering.

Vicky hung her head. "Yes, you are … back to Oz." If she wasn't careful she'd cry again. He'd think she was a wimp. Always boohooing.

"No," he said quickly. "I'm working here for a year … then, who knows?"

He was still clutching her hands. His face was serious now. He was looking at her with a kind of desperate hunger that had nothing to do with not having had any breakfast.

Vicky felt her heart flip. He moved closer. Then, suddenly, their arms were round one another and they were kissing and the whole world was spinning, a blizzard of stars exploding in her head.

When they drew apart, breathing ... breathless ... Luke said, "You've come to terms with it, then ... Sarah marrying Brian?"

"Brian?" she whispered against his mouth. "Who on earth's he?"

Outsider

Jill Eckersley

The beach was deserted. Sian pulled her woolly hat further down over her ears and wrapped her scarf around her face so that only her eyes and nose were showing. Brandy, her dog, came bounding up, dropped a piece of driftwood at her feet, and stood looking hopefully at her. Winter or summer, she loved the beach.

"OK, fetch!" said Sian, flinging the driftwood as far as she could along the sand, which felt as cold and hard as stone beneath her booted feet. Both sky and sea were the same chill, uninviting grey, and there were rims of ice around most of the rock pools. Even the waves looked lethargic, flopping over on to the shingle as though they could barely be bothered to break.

I know how they feel, Sian thought, as she strode along the sand, Brandy at her side. *There's nowhere lonelier than a seaside resort in winter. I'm beginning to wonder if it was really such a good idea coming to live here!*

Her father had been made redundant by the company he'd worked for since before Sian was born. When her parents asked her what she thought of the idea of buying and running a seaside guest-house with Dad's redundancy money, she'd been all for it. Moving house, helping her parents decorate and choose furnishings for the spare bedrooms had been hard work, but fun. Waiting for their first bookings had been exciting, and thanks to the hot summer, business had been excellent. Sian had been kept busy making beds, cleaning and tidying rooms, and serving meals, but there had been plenty of time for summer fun, too.

I just never stopped to think what it would be like here in winter, when all the holidaymakers had left, she thought miserably, kicking at a plastic detergent bottle that had been washed up by the last high tide, and trying hard not to cry. It was all right for Simon and Katie, her young brother and sister, who had school, football and Brownies to keep them happy. But what was *she* supposed to do for friends? Working at the guest-house meant that almost everyone she met was on holiday, here today and gone tomorrow. In the summer, it hadn't seemed to matter. The small seaside town was full of casual workers, people with summer jobs, people filling in time, ready to make friends with a newcomer like herself. She still got letters from Connie, a Dutch girl who had stayed with them. Kathleen, who'd had a summer job in town, wrote regularly from Ireland, but penfriends just weren't the same. How long is it since I went out and had a laugh with a crowd of mates, she thought bleakly. There's no one here for me now. No one … and nothing.

She closed her eyes for a moment and tried to imagine the beach as it had been in August. Kiddies building sandcastles, swimmers squealing as they plunged into the waves, old Joe the donkey-man, Dave who looked after the deck-chairs, Sue and Lisa, the students from London with holiday jobs in the seafront cafés, Pete from the caravan park and Tricia, his red-haired girlfriend. Tricia lived locally, but even she had gone away to college when the autumn came. The busy ice-cream kiosk, the little shop that sold everything from bread and aspirin to postcards, beach balls and fishing nets, the smell of chips and suntan oil...

When she opened her eyes again, the beach looked emptier than ever. The cafés were closed for the winter and the ice-cream kiosk was shuttered. Seabirds wheeled and cried overhead. Everyone had gone, except her – old Joe, Lisa, Sue, Pete and Tricia, Dave ... and Tim.

She wasn't supposed to be thinking about Tim. But the more she tried not to, the more his handsome, laughing face haunted her. He was a journalist on the local paper, based by the sea for the summer, "because that's where all the stories are. Not to mention the prettiest girls!" he had said, winking at her and making her blush. Sian had never quite understood what he saw in her. There were prettier and more sophisticated girls around, who she was sure would be more his type, but he singled her out from the start.

And what fun they'd had! He seemed to know everyone and be able to get in anywhere, with free tickets to concerts and most of the summer attractions.

"Perks of the job, honey," he'd said, ruffling her hair, when she'd asked him about it. He drove a smart red sports car, wore designer suits and Italian shoes, and seemed to work only when he felt like it. Sian had hoped against hope that when he went back to the paper's head office in the autumn, he'd keep in touch, perhaps even come down and see her for a weekend, but when she asked him, he just said "Oh, we'll see... It depends..." in the vaguest kind of way.

He hadn't telephoned her. She suffered agonies for about a fortnight, waiting for the call that never came. Then she plucked up the courage to phone him at the office. The first time, she asked for the newsdesk and got a bored-sounding girl who promised to pass on her name and number. The second time, she was put straight through to Tim. When she heard his voice her heart beat fast and the palms of her hands were wet.

"Tim? It's Sian!"

There was a moment's silence. I can't bear it, Sian thought. If he says "Sian who?" I'll just die, I know I will!

But he didn't. Instead, he gave the low

chuckle she remembered so well, that she had always found so sexy.

"Sian. Well, I never. How are you, honey? Nice of you to call!"

They had a short, awkward conversation. He said nothing about seeing her again, and Sian felt too shy to say all the things she longed to say, like why haven't you called me, and don't you want to see me again? I shouldn't have called him, she thought miserably, after they'd said good-bye. He's probably spinning the same lines to some other girl, right this moment.

Yet still, months later, she couldn't think of him without a pang of longing. Guys like Tim just didn't cross her path every day. Good-looking, charming, well off, he was every girl's dream. Things happened where Tim was. And now she was alone, and nothing was happening.

She felt tears of self-pity stinging the back of her eyes, and bent to pick up another stick to throw for Brandy. It was only when the dog had raced delightedly off along the beach in pursuit that Sian became aware that she was no longer alone. A young man in a green waxed jacket and wellingtons, his black curls ruffled by the winter wind, limped along the shingle just ahead of her.

Sian frowned. Why, it's Jake, she thought. Jake the Peg, as Tim called him. The dark young man with the limp had been on the fringes of the crowd all summer – on the beach, at the fairground, in the town, in the cafés – yet he had never really made friends with them. No one seemed to know very much about him, though they had found out that he was called Jake one day when they'd all been in the café, drinking Cokes and wondering how many of them could squeeze into Tim's car for a trip along the coast. Jake had come in, alone as usual, and limped up to the counter. One or two of the girls had looked at him with interest, but he didn't give any of them a second look. Instead, he sat at a table by himself and took no notice of anyone. Sue and Lisa exchanged glances, and Sue shrugged.

"Not exactly friendly, is he?" she muttered.

"Pity. He's cute!" Lisa whispered back.

"Shh, he'll hear you," said Sian, but Lisa and Sue didn't care.

"Your order, Jake," said Mrs Barrett, the café owner, bringing over a cup of tea and a plate of beans on toast.

Tim raised one blond eyebrow and grinned round at everyone.

"Jake," he said, hardly bothering to lower his voice. "I don't believe it, Jake the Peg!"

"Tim, shut up. That's cruel!" cried Sian, scandalized. She looked across at Jake but he was eating his beans on toast and reading his paper, giving no sign of having heard.

"Oh, leave it, honey, can't you take a joke?" Tim said, sounding bored.

Sian bit her lip. Tim often made her feel like that; naïve, a bit silly, as if, somehow, she was the one who'd done or said the wrong thing.

Sue and Lisa did try to find out more about Jake, but drew a blank. He seemed to be the original loner, and gradually, as more and more holidaymakers and summer workers came and went, Jake was forgotten.

And now here he was, just ahead of Sian on the otherwise deserted beach. Because of his limp, he walked much more slowly than she did and she soon caught up with him. Brandy sniffed around his boots and wagged her tail in her usual friendly way.

"Hi," said Sian, rather shyly, when it

became obvious that Jake wasn't going to say anything. As the only two people on a two-mile stretch of sand, she felt it was crazy for them to ignore one another. He looked surprised.

"Oh. Hi," he said brusquely.

"I ... er ... I haven't seen you down here before," Sian went on, feeling uncomfortable.

"No," he said, after a pause.

"I come here quite a lot. With my dog," Sian persevered. This is hard work, she thought. What's the matter with him, doesn't he like girls, or something? You'd think he'd be glad of someone to talk to on a day like today. I certainly am!

Then Brandy created a diversion by bringing a huge piece of driftwood over and dropping it, hopefully, at Jake's feet. He picked it up and threw it way down the shingle, far further than Sian could have managed. Brandy woofed in delight and went racing after it, bringing it back after a few moments and presenting it to Jake again. Sian couldn't help giggling.

"You've got a friend for life there," she said. "I hope you like dogs?"

"I love them," said Jake.

"Have you got one of your own?"

He shook his head.

Sian had been on the point of saying he was welcome to join her and Brandy on the beach any time, but she didn't like to. His replies were so curt and his dark face so unsmiling that she felt rather snubbed. Lisa and Sue were right, she thought huffily. He's not the friendly type.

"Well ... see you," she said awkwardly, whistling to Brandy, who after a last, longing look at Jake and the big piece of wood, trotted off beside her willingly enough.

Jake muttered something that could have been anything, hunched into his jacket and carried on along the shore in the opposite direction. Sian watched him go, feeling rather annoyed. Strange guy, she thought. He might have made a *bit* of effort to chat. Just my luck, the only guy my age I've seen in weeks, not bad-looking either, and he turns out to be some miserable, antisocial weirdo!

All the same, she thought as she walked home, there's something quite attractive about him. Not that he's really my type. Not like Tim...

Which is where I came in, she thought, depressed, as she went up the steps to the front door. I can't go on like this. Perhaps I should think again about college. There's always going to be a job for me here in the summer, when we're busy, but what about the winters?

It seemed a long time since she had rushed in, hoping there would be a message from Tim. There never was. How long had it taken her to realize that their summer romance had been just that to him – a summer fling, fun while it lasted, but soon forgotten? And she, Sian, had been just another girl.

"Oh, there you are, Sian," her mother said, sticking her head round the kitchen door. "You gave Brandy a good walk, love, thanks! Oh, by the way, someone called Tricia called for you. Tricia ... Brent?"

Sian frowned.

"Tricia Brent? Oh, Tricia! I wonder what she wants? I met her in the summer, Mum. She was going out with Pete from the caravan park. She lives up Vicarage Hill somewhere. She went off to college in October."

"Well, she's at home now," said her mum. "She said she wanted to invite you to a party on Saturday."

"A party!" Sian echoed, her spirits lifting at once. It was ages since she'd been to a party. It would be a chance to meet new people, make friends – hopefully – with people who lived locally and wouldn't all have to go back to college, or home, like the summer crowd.

A party is just what I need, Sian thought as she went upstairs to her bedroom, Tricia's telephone number in her hand. Then a thought sprang into her mind, unbidden. *I wonder if Jake will be there?*

Now what made me think of him, she thought, disturbed. He's not a party animal, for sure! I can't imagine him relaxing enough to boogie on down, or whatever! Still, I could at least ask Tricia if she knows who he is...

"Tricia? It's Sian, Sian Downes. Mum said something about a party?"

"Oh, hi, Sian. Yes, it's my eighteenth on Saturday. I'm not having a big do, but the crowd from college are coming down, why don't you come along? You're not busy, are you?"

"Chance would be a fine thing!" said Sian. "This place isn't exactly buzzing at this time of year, is it, Tricia?"

"You're telling me. Roll on the summer is what I say," said Tricia, with feeling. "Sunshine, blue skies, and loads of hunky, funky guys to give me a good time!"

"But what about Pete?" Sian asked.

"Pete? *Pete?* Do I know anybody called

Pete?" Tricia giggled. "He's ancient history, Sian. He was OK, but, well, out of sight is out of mind when it comes to summer romance!"

Sian wished she could be like Tricia, and take her romances lightly. Girls like Tricia, and guys like Tim, never got involved, never had their hearts broken, but she'd never been like that. It's much easier to fall in love than it is to fall out, she thought, as she rummaged through her wardrobe for something she could wear to Tricia's party. I know I'll probably never see Tim again, so why can't I just forget him? Why don't I say he's ancient history, like Tricia said about Pete?

The next day, when she took Brandy for her walk, she saw Jake again. He didn't speak, just nodded curtly. Oh well, Sian thought, if he doesn't want to be friendly...

She threw a piece of wood for Brandy. The dog rushed away, picked it up, worried it, and then gave a yelp of pain, dropped it, and came limping back along the shingle, her tail between her legs.

"Brandy? What's happened, what did you do?" Sian cried.

The dog sat down on the sand and began worrying at her right front paw.

"Here, let me look at that," came a

commanding voice.

It was Jake. Sian was so surprised that she let him take over, hoping Brandy wouldn't bite him. She was the sweetest-tempered of pets normally, but if she was in pain, and she hardly knew Jake...

But she need not have worried. Whining, Brandy rolled over on to her side and Jake took her sore paw in gentle hands.

"Mmm. It's a splinter, I can see it," he said. "What's her name?"

"Brandy," said Sian.

He stroked the dog's head soothingly. "Well, Brandy," he said, "I'm going to have to pull this splinter out, old girl. I'll try not to hurt you. One pull, and it'll be done, all right?"

Brandy looked up at him trustingly, her paw in his hands.

Sian watched apprehensively as he gave the splinter a good, hard tug. Brandy flinched, whimpered, but didn't attempt to bite. When Jake had finished, she licked her injured paw thoroughly and wagged her tail.

"There," said Jake, showing Sian a splinter about an inch long. "No wonder she was limping, poor old girl!"

"Thanks," said Sian gratefully. "It was really good of you!"

He shrugged and looked embarrassed.

"It was nothing," he said. "She's a lovely dog. Look, I've got to go now. I think she'll be OK. Bye."

He turned abruptly and limped away, leaving Sian gazing after him, feeling even more bewildered.

By the time she arrived on Saturday night, Tricia's party was in full swing. The house was ablaze with lights and she could hear the music halfway down the street.

"Sian! I'm glad you could make it!" Tricia, a glass of home-made punch in her hand and a huge "I'm 18" badge pinned to her dress, greeted her at the door. "Food and drink in the kitchen, dancing in the front room, coats upstairs in my room, there's a loo under the stairs and the bathroom's upstairs. Please don't go in my parents' bedroom or they'll murder me tomorrow..."

Still chattering, she led Sian into a room full of dancing couples. Lights flashed in time with the music. Three or four guys seemed to be deep in conversation about football, while a group of girls sat on the sofa.

"Let me introduce you to a few people," Tricia bawled above the noise of the music.

Soon, Sian's head was a whirl of new names, new faces, snippets of gossip, bright lights and dance music.

"Tricia," she began, "you don't know a guy named Jake something-or-other, do you? Dark, sort of gypsy-looking, walks with a limp?"

But when she looked round, Tricia had gone. Sian helped herself to another glass of punch and a handful of peanuts, and wondered why she was disappointed that Jake wasn't there? She didn't fancy him, after all. She wasn't sure she even liked him much and he'd made it all too obvious that he wasn't interested in her.

A fair-haired boy with glasses asked her to dance.

"Haven't seen you around before," he murmured. "What are you studying?"

"I'm not studying anything," replied Sian. "I live here!"

"Oh. A local," he said, in a tone of voice that made it sound as if she was a strange, exotic animal, or a visitor from the planet Zog. "What d'you do, then?"

"I work in my parents' guest-house," Sian said.

That seemed to silence him altogether. What a nerd, Sian thought. When the music stopped, she wasn't sorry to see him go. Tricia seemed to have disappeared, and when she went back to the girls she'd been introduced to, they were deep in conversation about a friend of theirs who was going out with one of the college lecturers. The football fans were still talking about football. Two couples were dancing and another couple were locked in one another's arms on the sofa. Sian stood by the stereo, feeling more lost and lonely than ever. I don't fit in, she thought.

She wandered into the kitchen, had a glass of water, made polite conversation with an older couple who said they were neighbours of Tricia's, and wished she could go home. So much for parties, she thought bitterly. If the guests weren't already paired off, they were students, with their own friends and their own lives. They weren't interested in hers.

Maybe it's me, she thought in the minicab on the way home. Perhaps there's something wrong with me and people just don't want to know. Perhaps I'm just boring, a boring little small-town girl.

Her parents were still up, watching the late-night movie, when she came in.

"Good party, love?" her dad asked casually.

For a moment, Sian was tempted to confide

in them, cry on her mum's shoulder just as if she was a little girl again. After all, her parents had had to settle down in a new town too. But then, they had each other.

"Lovely, thanks," she said, her head held high and she climbed the stairs to bed. Not even to her mum and dad did she want to admit how wretched she felt.

It was only later still, just before she fell asleep, that she remembered she hadn't found out any more about Jake.

He was there on the beach the next day. Once again he was alone. But this time, wonder of wonders, he actually looked up and smiled at her. He had a nice smile, too, Sian noticed. Brandy gave him a woof of greeting and he fondled her silky brown ears.

"Hello," he said, "how's Brandy today?"

"Fine," Sian returned. "Her paw's much better, thanks to you!"

Silence fell and Sian began to feel embarrassed.

"Walking the dog again, are you?" he said.

Sian nodded.

"She loves the beach," she said.

"So do I," said Jake. "Even in winter. Especially in winter, when all the trippers have gone and it's just me and the sea and the sky."

"It's my first winter here," Sian confided. "It's … quiet, isn't it?"

He gave a sudden snort of laughter that made her jump.

"Aye, it's quiet, all right. Don't you like that?"

"Well … it's a bit lonely. But I went to a party last night and met a few people, you know…"

Was it her imagination, or did he look ever so slightly disappointed?

"Oh. Well, you'll be all right, then," he said, rather bleakly.

"What on earth do you mean?"

He hunched into his coat again, kicked out at a larger-than-usual pebble, and shrugged.

"Just that some people are party types and some aren't," he said.

What a strange, moody guy he is, Sian thought. But she wasn't going to let him get away with it, not this time!

"I don't think that's true," she objected. "Last night, I was a party type, if you want to call it that; today I'm a walking on the beach with my dog type! It depends how I feel!"

He flashed her his unexpected smile again.

"Fair enough," he said. "I don't like parties

much myself. Full of trendies and posers, showing off their fancy clothes."

Sian couldn't help glancing at his ripped jeans and grubby jacket. She didn't say anything, but when she looked up again their eyes met and suddenly, they both burst out laughing. He held out his hand.

"I'm Jake Stratton."

"Sian Downes."

They shook hands solemnly. Somehow it seemed quite natural, after that, for them to walk on up the beach together.

"Have you always lived here, Jake?" Sian asked.

"Yes. I work at the wildlife sanctuary. Have you been there?"

Sian hadn't, although she'd seen a leaflet about it in the guest-house.

"What do you do?" she asked him, fascinated. "Take care of the animals?"

"Yes, and the birds. We've got some quite rare seabirds, and people bring injured animals to us, too, mostly hedgehogs and squirrels and things like that. We had a badger once, and we quite often get abandoned fox cubs. Pets find their way to us now and again, too. You know, people leave, move house, and leave their dogs and cats to fend for themselves, especially if they're old or sick..."

Sian gasped.

"How could anyone be so cruel? Brandy's part of our family, and so are Topsy and Sheba, our cats! We'd never leave them, never!"

Jake shrugged.

"Well, people do, and worse. We've had animals brought in with wounds from shotgun pellets, birds half-strangled by abandoned fishing-lines, a swan with a broken wing that some kids were tormenting..."

"Oh, no!"

"Oh, yes. People can be dead cruel, Sian!"

Sian bit her lip.

"And ... and are you able to help all the animals?"

"Most of them, yes, I'm glad to say. Some don't make it. But we do what we can. It's what makes the job worthwhile."

"I think that's fantastic. I'd love to work with animals," said Sian warmly.

"Bet you wouldn't. Not if it meant turning out of your nice warm bed at four in the morning to look after a trapped vixen and her cubs!"

"I would, if I had to!" Sian insisted. He can

be arrogant sometimes, she thought, but he's still the most interesting guy I've met for ages, far more interesting than the boys at Tricia's party last night.

"You should come down some time. I'd like to show you round," Jake said.

Their eyes met. His were very dark, with a watchful expression, as if he found it hard to trust people. He's a bit like a wild animal himself, Sian thought. The type you could stroke, or the type that would bite you? She wasn't sure...

"Listen, I've got to go. Mum will be expecting me," she said.

There was a tiny pause. Please, Sian thought. Please ask to see me again.

She was surprised how much she wanted him to.

"I'll see you, then," he said. And then, almost as though he could read her thoughts, he smiled his devastating smile again and added "Tomorrow?"

Sian nodded, her heart singing.

"Tomorrow," she repeated. She could feel herself blushing and she covered her sudden shyness by calling Brandy to heel.

Sian was woken, in the middle of the night,

by a violent storm. Rain lashed against her bedroom windows and she could hear the wind moaning around the house, rattling the windowframes and making the old trees in the garden creak alarmingly.

Brr, she thought, snuggling down under her duvet, I'm glad I'm not out in that! Peering at the illuminated dial on her bedside clock, she saw that it was half-past four.

She was yawning when she came down to breakfast, where Simon and Katie, her brother and sister, were squabbling over the last Weetabix.

"I want it! You can have Bran Flakes!" whined Katie.

"'S not fair! Don't like Bran Flakes," sulked Simon.

"Quiet, you two," said Mrs Downes, pouring boiling water into the teapot. "Are you all right, Sian? You look a bit pale!"

Sian nodded as she helped herself to toast and marmalade.

"I'm OK, I just had a bad night," she said. "The wind kept me awake."

Her mother looked serious.

"I know. It was quite a storm. Your dad's gone out to make sure the fences haven't blown down, or the TV aerial. It's still pouring down out there."

Sian listened to the wind and then peered out of the kitchen window at the dark grey, angry-looking clouds scudding across the sky. Looks like we're in for more rain, she thought with a sinking heart. That means no walks on the beach for Brandy. And no Jake.

She realized how much she had been looking forward to seeing him again.

Her father came in, wet and windswept, in an orange cagoule and wellingtons.

"There's no damage that I can see," he reported, "but it still looks bad."

The storm continued to rage for most of the day, confining Sian and Brandy to the house. She did slip out for half an hour at about four, when the rain stopped, but it was almost dark by then and all she could do was give Brandy a quick run round the block. There was no sign of Jake.

Maybe he'll be there again tomorrow, she thought.

Her parents switched on the TV for the mid-evening news. Sian listened with half an ear while she read a magazine. It was only when the newsreader said "Halbury-on-Sea" that she sat up with a jerk.

"Did he say Halbury? *Here?* What's happened?" she cried.

"Ssh!" said her father.

"...a threat to holiday beaches, and to wildlife," came the newsreader's voice. "Hundreds of seabirds, their feathers clogged with oil, are being washed up on the beaches. The RSPCA, the Royal Society for the Protection of Birds, and local conservation groups have been alerted, and are mounting a rescue operation."

Sian didn't even hear the rest of the broadcast.

"Dad, what happened?" she repeated. "Where did the oil come from?"

"A tanker ran aground in the storm," her father said. "They're hoping she'll float off on the next high tide, but one of her tanks was holed and there was a bad oil leak, they said."

"Oh, Dad! Our lovely beach! And the birds!"

"Don't worry, love, they'll clear it up," said her mother comfortingly.

But Sian wasn't listening. "Local conservation groups" the newsreader had said. That had to mean the sanctuary where Jake worked. She'd go down the beach, tomorrow, and find him. Perhaps she could even help.

By the next day the ferocious wind had died

down, it had stopped raining, and a pale, watery sun had come out.

"I'm going down to the beach, Mum," Sian called, pulling on her wellies and her oldest, scruffiest jacket. No use wearing anything decent if it was going to get covered in oil. She knew Jake well enough by now to realize he would be more impressed if she looked businesslike and ready to help, recalling, with a grin, his scorn for "posers in fancy clothes". She pulled on a hat and gloves and set off, leaving Brandy gazing mournfully after her.

"Sorry, old girl, not this time," she told her. "Mum doesn't want oily paw-marks all over the house!"

There were a handful of sightseers on the beach, plus two vans from the RSPCA and several uniformed inspectors. There was also a battered white Transit van, driven by a very tall man in oilskins with a beard and marked "Halbury Wildlife Rescue". Sian ran round to the back of the van, and there, with a pile of flat cardboard cartons and a stack of black plastic rubbish sacks, was Jake.

"Jake," she said urgently.

He looked up, unsmiling as usual, and her heart turned right over. What's the matter with me? she thought. This guy is scruffy, moody, arrogant, not my type at all...

"Hello," he said. "What are you doing here? Come to stand around and stare, like those pillocks up there, have you?" He jerked a contemptuous thumb in the direction of the little knot of sightseers at the edge of the beach.

"No, I have not!" said Sian indignantly. "I've come to help! There must be something I can do, Jake. Anything at all, just tell me!"

He suddenly relaxed and smiled.

"I'm sorry," he said gently. "You mean it, don't you? You really mean it."

"Of course I do! I've told you, I'll do anything."

He was looking thoughtful when one of the RSPCA inspectors came round to the back of the van.

"Ready with those boxes, Jake? And the bags?"

"Not quite," said Jake. "Ron, this is my friend Sian. She wants to help, but she has no experience with birds at all."

There must be *something* I can do, Sian thought. She had never felt so helpless, or so useless. The RSPCA inspector smiled at her.

"Rescuing seabirds is a job for the experts,

really, Sian," he said. "There's no simple way to catch a wild bird. They're already shocked and stressed. If you don't know what you're doing, you can easily damage their wings and make things worse! We can't rescue them all, we just have to collect as many, as carefully as we can, and take them away to be cleaned up. I'm not sure…"

"She could do the boxes for me," said Jake suddenly. "Then I could go out after the birds."

The inspector's brow cleared.

"Good idea," he said. "Show her what to do, Jake, and then join us down at the waterline, OK?"

Jake nodded and proceeded to show Sian how to fold the flat cardboard into a box big enough to carry an oil-clogged seabird. There were dozens of boxes.

"Sure you can manage?" Jake said.

"Course I can," said Sian firmly. It wasn't quite what she had imagined, being stuck in the back of this rusty, slightly smelly old van, folding cardboard boxes. But if it helped Jake…

It was more difficult than it looked. The cardboard was stiff, wouldn't bend as it should, tore at her fingernails and left her hands sore, scratched and so cold she could barely feel them. Her eyes watered with the cold, her nose ran, and her feet felt like blocks of ice. But she persevered, grimly determined to prove to Jake that she could do a good job.

"Well done, Sian!"

Jake inspected the pile of boxes Sian had put together and stacked neatly on the sand. He was filthy, his waxed jacket covered in sticky, smelly oil. In his arms was an equally oily guillemot, its beady eyes peering out in fear. Ron, the inspector, opened one of the boxes wide and Jake slipped the bird in, closing it and putting it safely in the van.

"Will it be OK?" Sian wanted to know.

Jake shrugged.

"It's alive," he said. "Once the oil gets into their feathers it destroys their natural water-proofing and they get waterlogged. When they try to clean their feathers they swallow the oil and it poisons them. That bird is chilled and wet and shocked and will have to be stabilized before we even try to clean it up."

"Poor thing," said Sian. "I hope it makes it!"

"It's one of the lucky ones," Jake insisted. "There are dozens of dead birds down there — mostly guillemots, a few razorbills, even a puffin. There's nothing we can do for them. We just have to do our best for the survivors."

"Yes," said Sian, picking up yet another cardboard carton to assemble. Somehow, seeing Jake's dedication made her feel better. Even though her fingers and toes were freezing, she wasn't going to give up.

And she didn't. She folded carton after carton while Jake and Ron brought dozens of frightened, oily birds from the beach to the van. When it was full, Jake's boss drove it away to the sanctuary, leaving Jake and Sian, cold, wet, dirty and exhausted, at the top of the beach. Sian was so tired that she was almost in tears.

"Look at it," said Jake in disgust, wiping his filthy hands on an even filthier rag he'd rescued from beneath the van's front seat. At the water's edge, where he and Sian had thrown sticks for Brandy just the other day, were streams and puddles of thick, brown, oozing oil. Some of the helpers had collected up the dead birds and left them in sad little heaps, waiting to be bulldozed away by the Council workmen.

"It makes me sick to see what we're doing to beautiful creatures like seabirds," said Jake passionately. "They should be up there, out there, flying free, not lying dead on some filthy beach, clogged up with oil!"

Sian felt hot angry tears spill from her eyes and pour down her cold cheeks. She didn't even know why she was crying. For the poor, dead seabirds? For Jake? Or for herself?

She gave a huge, choking sob, unable to stop herself. Oh, no, she thought, what will Jake think, he'll laugh at me...

But, to her amazement, he looked at her, raised one eyebrow, put his dirty, oil-stained arm around her equally grubby shoulders, and pulled her close to him. When she felt his lips just lightly brush the top of her head, Sian thought she must be dreaming.

"Jake?" she said, questioningly, looking up at him.

"You did a great job. You mustn't let it get to you," he said huskily. "We'll save some of the birds, Sian, I promise. That's all any of us can do. And you did your bit."

Slowly, very slowly, he bent his head until his lips met hers. His mouth was cold, his fingers cold in her hair, but there was a warmth and sweetness in his kiss that melted Sian's heart. She clung to him.

"Jake," she repeated, wonderingly. Kissing him felt right. It felt like coming home. Her heart too full for words, she snuggled up to him, resting her face against his chest. Everything suddenly seemed simple. She'd been lonely, looking for friendship, for love, and she'd found them both, in one guy. In Jake – moody, passionate, yet tender and caring, all at once.

"Sian?" he murmured.

"Mmm?" she replied, looking up at him dreamily.

"You look like a chimney-sweep. There's oil all over your face!" he said, grinning.

The romantic spell broken, Sian couldn't help laughing. What I want most of all, at this moment, she decided, is a nice, hot bath! And Jake could do with one, too. She realized, with a shock, that she didn't even know where he lived.

"I live at the sanctuary," he told her, when she asked. "I've got a bedsitter there. My dad died when I was a kid and I never got on with my step-dad, so when I heard there was a job going with accommodation, I was there like a shot! I spent half my time up there with the animals anyway, even when I was at school."

"It sounds lonely," said Sian, thinking, with a pang, of her own happy family life. She sometimes had rows with her parents, and

Simon and Katie could be complete brats, but she wouldn't want to be without them.

"No lonelier than I was before," said Jake bitterly. "'Cos of this" – he touched his lame leg – "I never fitted in at school, never could play football like the other lads. Maybe that's why I liked animals so much. Animals and birds don't care if you're lame, if you're different..."

Sian realized, with a shock, that she had forgotten all about Jake's disability. It seemed a part of him, somehow, and it hadn't slowed him up when he was rescuing the sea-birds.

"Come home with me now," she suggested, half shyly. "I'd like you to meet my mum and dad, and I'm dying for a hot bath!"

He hesitated for a moment and then said, "OK, if you're sure they won't mind the mess I'm in!"

She laughed.

"You don't look any worse than I do!"

They were walking up the steps to the promenade, hand in hand, when a sandy-haired man in his thirties with a camera suddenly approached them.

"Excuse me," he said, "are you part of the rescue team?"

"Who wants to know?" enquired Jake coolly.

"I'm Sam Johnson, from the *Post*," said the photographer. "I've been sent down here with one of our reporters to cover the rescue story. Here, Tim, over here! These two were involved in the rescue operation!"

Sian froze, and her heart began to thump. Tim, the photographer had said, and she knew the *Post* was Tim's paper! Tim, her summer romance, the handsome blond journalist with the smart suits and fancy car. Tim, who had almost broken her heart. Tim, whom she'd thought she would never see again. Oh no, she thought, I don't want to talk to him! I don't want him even to see me!

But it was too late. An all-too-familiar figure in a beige coat swung round to face her and Jake. Tim took a few steps forward and then his eyes widened in recognition.

"Sian, honey! I don't believe it! Great to see you, it's been ages!"

"Yes, it has. Hello, Tim," said Sian weakly, not daring to look at Jake. Would he remember Tim? Had he seen them together in the café, heard Tim sniggering and calling him Jake the Peg?

Tim was smiling the smile she remembered

so well; rueful, charming, the smile that had made her knees feel weak.

"I should've called you, shouldn't I, sweetheart? Forgive me?" he said, and his voice was like a caress. Not waiting for Sian's reply, he went on, "This is fantastic! You're a proper little heroine, aren't you, rescuing all these birds. It'll make a fantastic story, our readers will love it. A pretty local girl on a mercy mission! It might even make the front page. What d'you think, Sam?"

The photographer shrugged.

"Could do. We could try it. But..."

He and Tim looked at one another meaningfully, and Tim laughed.

"That's a point. Sian, lovey, you're not really looking your most glamorous, are you?"

Sian felt Jake let go of her hand abruptly. Cold, confused, and weary to the bone, Sian just looked at Tim.

"No," she said. "I've been on the beach all day. I was planning to go home and have a bath..."

"Oh, come on, sweetie, it won't take long," Tim wheedled. "I can see the headlines now. 'Local Heroine Saves Wildlife!'"

"But I didn't!" said Sian. "All I did was fold

cardboard boxes, if you really want to know."

But Tim obviously wasn't listening.

"What we really need," he said, "is a shot of you with one of the birds. You know, actually cradling it in your arms, something like that. Any birds around, mate?" he said, addressing Jake for the first time.

Jake looked at him, unsmiling.

"Only dead ones," he said.

"What? Oh … oh. No, that won't do. What happened to the live ones, the ones you rescued?"

"They've been taken to the sanctuary," Sian explained. "They're in shock, you see, they need to have their strength built up before they can even be cleaned up properly."

"Where is this sanctuary?" Tim asked. "Could we go there, get a shot of you carrying a seagull?"

"They're not seagulls…" Sian began.

Then Jake broke in.

"No, you can't," he said through gritted teeth. "Didn't you hear what Sian said? These birds are in shock! They need rest and quiet and care, and even then they might not survive. You can't just pick them up and play with them for the sake of some stupid newspaper story! They're not toys, they're living creatures! They deserve a bit of respect! But what would you know about that, you…"

Both Tim and Sam the photographer had stepped back a pace or two. For the first time since Sian had known him, Tim actually looked flustered.

"OK, OK. Keep your hair on. I was only asking," he muttered.

"Well, the answer's no!" said Jake. The unsmiling look was back on his face and he refused to meet Sian's eyes.

"I'm off," he said suddenly. "It sounds like you two old friends have quite a bit of catching up to do! I'll see you around, Sian!"

He turned and hurried away, his limp suddenly much more obvious.

This can't be happening, Sian thought. Tim seemed to have recovered his composure and was gazing after Jake with a sarcastic smile.

"That's Jake the Peg, isn't it?" he said. "Quite a firebrand, isn't he? Come on, Sian, how about a photo? Just a quick one, then later maybe we could get together for a drink, what d'you say?"

But Sian was watching the hunched

figure in the grubby jacket, limping away along the oil-polluted beach, his dark hair blowing in the winter wind, looking lonelier than anyone she had ever seen. Then she looked at Tim, smiling confidently in his smart designer outfit, and came to life.

"No," she almost shouted. "No, I don't want to be in the paper! And I don't want to see you again, Tim! Not ever!"

"But Sian..." Tim began pleadingly.

Sian began to run, hampered by her oil-clogged wellingtons, but suddenly feeling very sure, very free. How could I ever have thought I was in love with that idiot, she thought as she ran, Jake's worth ten of him! It's not clothes and cars and being in with the in-crowd that matter. It's kindness, and caring, and all the things that Jake knows all about and Tim would never understand in a thousand years!

She had almost reached the rocks.

"Jake! Come back!" she shouted, but the wind tore her voice away.

Gasping, stumbling, slipping on oil and seaweed, she went on following the dark figure in the waxed jacket.

"Jake!" she screamed, losing her footing, almost falling.

He had heard her. He turned, hesitated for a moment, and then, very slowly, began picking his way back across the rocks towards her.

"Oh, Jake," Sian sobbed, "please come back. Don't leave me..."

A moment later, two strong arms were around her, holding her tight. She looked up at him. Were those real tears in his eyes, or was he just cold?

"I thought ... I thought..." he muttered, against her hair.

"I know what you thought," Sian choked, half-laughing, half-crying. "But you're wrong. There's nothing between Tim and me now, nothing at all!"

He put his hand gently under her chin and tilted her face up to his.

"You're sure?"

She nodded.

"It's you, Jake. Only you!"

Their lips met ... and held ... and clung.

Suddenly, it felt like summer.

Love by e-mail

Amber Vane

You have three messages announced the flashing icon on the computer screen. Idly, Tess clicked her mouse to check her e-mails. The first was from her area supervisor offering a training course in spreadsheets. She deleted it. The second was from her friend Angie in Accounts, advising her to look out of the window at exactly ten o'clock because that was when the hunky new window cleaner would be at her floor. The third was anonymous. The subject? *VALENTINE*.

Tess sat up a little straighter as she clicked to see the message. So far, this Valentine's Day had been a disappointment. Oh, sure, she received a couple of cards through the post – what the IT department always referred to as the "Snail Mail". But she knew for a fact that one of them had to have come from her mother. Only she knew which Everton player was actually her favourite –

and only she would have bothered to cut out his face and stick it on to the big red satin heart. Come to think of it, only a mother would buy a card with a big red satin heart on it.

The other card, she was fairly certain, was from her brother Freddie, now at university in Newcastle. She was no Miss Marple, but the Newcastle postmark had been a big clue. And while it was sweet of Freddie to think of her, it was hardly romantic.

It was not as if she was expecting anything special. Tess didn't have a boyfriend or even a prospect of one, unless you counted gorgeous Gavin from Housing. Now, he was someone she fancied a lot. The trouble was, she could never be certain quite what he thought of her. He was friendly enough and had even asked her to dance once or twice when they fetched up at the same parties. But that was it.

So she was intrigued as the mysterious missive unravelled on to the screen. It was more like a riddle than a love poem, though:

Press on my heartstrings
Press on my key

To download my message
Click your launch facility

Tess frowned. What on earth was a launch facility? Her boss, Marion, appeared in the doorway that connected her office to Tessa's area. "Can you get these press notices out, priority, please?" she asked.

Still staring at her screen, Tess reached out her hand to take the sheaf of papers. Marion handed them to her and added with heavy sarcasm, "I did say priority, Tess. Which means this century. Preferably, this lunchtime."

"Fine, don't worry," Tess muttered, still staring. As soon as Marion was safely back in her office, Tess tapped a number rapidly into the telephone. "Hello, is that Computer Services? Great — can someone come urgently, please? I think my machine's got a bug." She always said that when she wanted attention fast. For some reason, computer people got really upset at the idea that there might be a virus in the system.

Within minutes, Barry was by her side — thin, pale, earnest-looking Barry, whose glasses always seemed to be sliding down his nose, and whose shock of long hair was for ever dangling over his eyes. "Sir Galahad at your service," he announced with a salute. "What is it this time? Paper stuck again? Or perhaps you just forgot to put any paper in? Or have you been too free with your delete button? I've warned you about that before."

"Very funny," snapped Tess. "The best thing you ever showed me was the Undo key. And sometimes I wish I could use it on certain people."

"Oh, you couldn't do that," Barry told her severely. "It only works with this software package. Most humans are programmed differently."

"Yeah – humans," Tess retorted. "Now are you going to help me or not?"

She showed Barry the Valentine message and he clicked and tapped a few times, waited, and soon a vast landscape began to fill Tess's screen. It was a forest scene, with trees and bushes, flowers and berries. As they gazed awestruck at the lavish computer image, the whole picture began to move. A squirrel scampered up a tree; a bush burst into bloom; a bee began to buzz round a cluster of blossom. Eventually two birds appeared in two different trees, then flew to a nest in another and their beaks touched in a kiss.

Tess was speechless. Barry gave a low whistle. "Someone went to a lot of trouble over this," he told her. "Even if the guy knows something about computers it takes ages to set up such a complicated image."

"No, it doesn't make sense," Tess taunted, mystified. "Guys who spend all day booting up their floppies just aren't romantic, are they?"

Tess regretted the words the moment she'd spoken them. Barry winced as though he'd been stung and she realized she'd done it again – upset someone with her careless words. It wasn't as though she ever intended to, but she always seemed to speak before she thought things through properly.

"I'm sorry, Barry," she muttered. "I didn't mean it the way it came out. It was a joke, right?"

Barry shrugged. "We may look tough and manly, but inside we're soft as jelly," he told her. As he left, he tripped over a pile of newspapers by her desk and sent a cup of coffee flying.

Tess couldn't help giggling. Barry was

well-meaning, she supposed, even if he was a bit of a wimp. Then her eye strayed back to the richly embellished picture on her screen. Who could it be? she pondered dreamily. Who could possibly have sent such an elaborate, meaningful Valentine?

"Morning, darling!" That was Dominic, one of the press officers who worked for Marion. He was quite good-looking, if you liked smarmy slickness. But Tess and Angie had long ago agreed that he was one of those blokes who just thought too much of themselves, and expected every girl to find him as irresistible as he found himself.

Now, she looked up at Dominic's grinning face leering at her over the top of her computer screen. "Morning. I'm busy. 'Bye," she answered.

"Oh, come on, Tess," protested Dominic. "No need to be like that. It is Valentine's Day, you know. And I've got you something." From behind his back he produced a single red rose.

"Where did you nick that from?" asked Tess, unimpressed. She'd noticed a huge arrangement of red flowers in the foyer that morning.

Dominic looked hurt. "I wish you'd get

the message," he said, fixing her with his eyes. For a brief moment, she wondered if he was referring to the wonderful electronic Valentine. She supposed it was just possible it had come from him. But no – it didn't seem likely. He probably meant something quite different.

"You really shouldn't curl up and spit every time anyone's nice to you," Dominic went on. "I don't know what your problem is, Tess, but sometimes I think you just don't know how to handle people who want to get close."

To her annoyance, Tess felt her face burning with a sudden blush. It was true that, deep down, Tess felt a bit shy and unsure of herself and that was often when she made her flippant, sharp remarks. But could Dominic be right, that it was all a way of making sure people kept their distance?

"I really think you and I could be great together," he was saying. "If you'd just give it a chance. I've always fancied you, you know, Tess."

That convinced her. Dominic was not the subtle type. "You fancy everything that moves – and some that don't," she pointed out.

He looked nonplussed for a minute. Then brightened. "You're just complimenting me on my fantastic ability to see the good in everyone," he said. "So there's a chance for me, after all. Will I see you at the Valentine Disco tonight?"

"Not if I see you first," Tess muttered. Undeterred, Dominic sauntered away, whistling. She noticed that he was hiding several more red roses behind his back, and was distributing them among all the girls in the office.

Ever since the local authority had first introduced it for all their employees four years before, the Humberlee and District Council Valentine Disco had become something of a tradition. It was held in the vast Town Hall banqueting suite, with a huge area for dancing and an upper gallery where you could sit at tables and watch the action.

"Do you think we're a bit over the top?" Angie asked Tess anxiously as they crushed their way into the crowded hall. They were both wearing tiny, slinky minidresses, Angie's in a silky grey to complement her blonde hair and Tess's in a startling black and white geometric pattern, which suited her starkly cut, dead straight dark bob. Both girls teetered on impossibly high heels, Angie's silver and Tess's bright red.

"Not at all," Tess assured her. "You want to be noticed, don't you?"

"I should think you'll be noticed in Australia, the way you're got up," commented a familiar voice right behind them. Tess swung round to see Barry grinning at her. "In fact, the shoes alone are so loud I'm surprised they haven't been invited on to the stage to test the sound equipment."

"So who asked you?" Tess demanded wearily. "Besides, at least we've made an effort. You've still got your breakfast on your tie."

"No I haven't — that's the jazzy pattern," Barry told her. "Don't you like it?"

"It suits you," Tess replied shortly, then looked away as she saw the hurt in Barry's eyes.

"Why do you always have to put guys down like that?" Angie asked. "I mean, I agree he's no Brad Pitt, but he's a nice enough bloke. No need to be nasty, Tess."

Inside, Tess agreed with Angie. She

wished she hadn't been so unkind. But, somehow, she couldn't quite admit it. "Oh, he'll get over it," she said airily. "And we certainly don't want to be stuck with nerdy Barry and his computer cronies all night."

Just then, Dominic appeared from nowhere and took her arm.

"Aha! My favourite girl!" he greeted her, whirling her across the floor without even asking if she wanted to dance. "I can tell that you've been waiting for me, just like I've been waiting for you." Tess couldn't tell from his wide-eyed, earnest expression whether or not he was teasing her. She decided to play safe.

"Er, Dominic, hello?" she said patiently as they were dancing. "This is planet real calling planet make-believe. And no – it wasn't me waiting for you. You must have me confused with some other girl. A girl with different taste in men."

Dominic pulled her to him as the music ended. "If you don't loosen up, Tess, you'll never know what your taste in men is," he said, "because no one will dare come close enough for you to see. Thanks for the dance."

Speechless, Tess watched him as he disappeared into the crowd. Then she gasped with pain as Angie dug her hard in the ribs. "Look out, at ten o'clock!" she hissed, directing Tess to a figure making his way towards them from the left. "It's Gavin — gorgeous Gavin! And he's making straight for you!"

And sure enough, there was Gavin, looking even more hunky than usual in tight black jeans and a red and black check shirt with three top buttons undone. "Tess!" he greeted her. "Good to see you. Fancy a dance?"

Fortunately it was too noisy and too crowded for Tess to be expected to answer. Speechless with excitement she followed Gavin on to the floor. She soon forgot her shyness. Gavin was a great dancer, the music was fast with a hard, driving beat, and she flung herself into wilder and wilder gyrations, matched by Gavin's own athletic movements.

At last, the music changed to a slow number. Smiling, Gavin pulled her close. "You really are some dancer," he murmured. "I like a girl who knows what to do with her body." As they swayed together to the soft, smoochy ballad, Gavin ran his hands up and down her back, then rested them on her narrow waist. "And what a body," he murmured appreciatively. "You really are something, Tess."

For the rest of the dance, as they moved sensuously round the floor, her head pressed against his chest, his arms tightening round her, Tess felt as though she was floating. It was all coming true, she thought. Gavin did like her after all. Maybe – oh, maybe, she thought ecstatically – it was Gavin who'd sent her the Valentine this morning. Yes, after all, he obviously liked her. And who else could it possibly have been?

"Fancy a stroll outside?" he murmured as the music ended. He took her hand and led her through the back of the hall to the garden. It was dark and deserted and rather cold. Tess shivered and Gavin put his arm round her.

"I'll keep you warm," he promised, with a glint in his eye. He steered her towards a bench, sat her down and immediately began to kiss her. But these were not the soft, romantic, tender kisses she had dreamed about, longed for for so long. Gavin's mouth was hard, almost brutal, crushing her lips with an urgent, impatient hunger that frightened her.

"No," she said in a strangled voice, pushing him away. Gavin stopped abruptly and stared at her.

"What do you mean?" he asked, clearly mystified. "Isn't this what you wanted?"

"Er – no, I mean, yes. Oh – I don't know. I didn't expect..." She stared at him wildly. She expected, half feared, that he might be angry. "I'm sorry, Gavin, I've got to go back now."

"Please yourself," Gavin shrugged. As she bolted back into the warmth and noise of the crowded party, she was aware that he hadn't followed her, hadn't even bothered to watch her after she'd torn away from him.

Back in the main hall she threaded her way through the crush to find Angie. She was dancing with Rod, one of the press officers. Desperately, she signalled to Angie using their secret code. Two squeezes on the arm followed by one plunk on your own bra strap meant: *Meet you in the Ladies right away. Emergency!*

"What's got into you?" Angie demanded crossly. "Things were just beginning to get going with Rod just now."

"Oh, he'll still be there in a minute," Tess said dismissively. She gave her friend a quick, fairly accurate account. "I can't understand it," she finished with a sob. "I wasn't a person to him at all, he was just using me. It was horrible." And then, to her horror, she found she was crying, really crying hard. She felt as though her heart was breaking.

Alarmed, Angie put her arm round her friend. Tess almost never cried. "Hey, it'll be OK," she tried to comfort her. "He's just a guy, remember? And you weren't even going out with him. Sounds like you've had a lucky escape."

Tess, who was slumped in front of the mirror, raised her head from her arms and looked at her friend. "No, you don't understand – it's not just Gavin, it's me. I'll never get a boyfriend, never. I don't know how to. I mean, I thought Gavin liked me and I got it all wrong. I must give out the wrong signals or something."

"Yes, I think you do," Angie agreed unexpectedly. "Not just to Gavin – after all, you hardly know him. It's the idea of him you liked, not the guy. I was thinking about all those other people you scare off, without giving them a chance. How can you tell if someone's right for you, if you never give them a chance?"

Tess didn't reply. She was feeling too miserable. And, deep down, she had a suspicion that Angie was right. She hid her shyness and awkwardness with wise-cracking remarks and cruel retorts. And then, when she did decide to take someone seriously, he turned out to have no interest in her at all. What a mess!

"Listen, you've had a shock," said Angie. "You need a drink. Let's go and grab a table."

While they were sipping their Red Hot Valentines – cocktails made of Cherryade and lime with a piece of lemon stuck in the top – Tess clutched Angie's arm and pointed down to the dance floor. There was Gavin, snaking sensually in time to the music with another smiling, laughing, mini-skirted girl.

"Hmm – that's Cheryl from Personnel," commented Angie, trying to make light of Tess's obvious distress. "What do you want me to do, kill her or warn her?"

"Oh, nothing," said Tess, her voice trembling. "I feel so – so worthless. I just wish that I could meet some really nice, gentle, romantic guy who wanted me for me."

"There's Dominic," suggested Angie. "He's

pretty keen on you. After himself, of course, I'd say you were fairly high on his list."

"I don't mean him," scoffed Tess. "It's no good the wrong guy being keen. And believe me, he is the wrong guy, Angie."

"Let's face it, you are choosy," Angie told her. "It's like – when you don't fancy someone, you really let them know it."

"That's because I'm honest," Tess said earnestly. "If it's not the right man, I'd rather have no man." She added dreamily, "He must be out there somewhere. A loving, tender guy who doesn't mind talking about his feelings, doesn't mind admitting that he cries sometimes and feels lonely sometimes. Someone I could really talk to and trust and not have to put on an act with."

"Well, maybe you should advertise," Angie suggested. "If you're so sure of what you want."

"That's an idea." Tess brightened a little. "I just might. What do you think? The local paper?" She looked gloomy again. "No, I might attract all kinds of losers. I need some kind of safety clause to screen out the ones who aren't right."

"I know," said Angie, excitedly. "Why not do it on the Internet? That way, you don't even have to meet anyone. You just send messages."

"Brilliant!" said Tess, cheering up. "And that way, I'll have to think before I speak, won't I? So I'll really be able to give people a chance." Her face fell again. "But I don't know how to do it, do I? And I couldn't possibly ask one of the cyber-freaks in Computer Support. It'd be all round the building before you could say megabyte."

She rolled her eyes over to the next table, where Barry was just about to sit down with a couple of his friends. He gave her a cheery wave, then turned very pointedly to his mates and started talking to them intently.

"Phew, narrow escape," said Tess. "You see what I mean, Angie. Those guys are just a bunch of techno-hacks. The closest they come to kissing is by keeping their fingers pressed down on the capital X on the keyboard."

"I do think you're a bit hard on Barry," Angie told her. "He's a perfectly nice guy really."

"Well, maybe," Tess conceded. "But that still doesn't mean I want him knowing that I'm about to become a Virtual Lonely Heart.

So what do I do?"

"I'll help you," offered Angie. "I just did a course. We'll post up a message on the Loveline Bulletin, spelling out exactly the kind of guy you'd like to meet, with a few details about yourself, of course. And let's just see what happens."

Tess glanced down at the dance floor, where Gavin was now holding Cheryl very close, his hands slithering up and down her back. She suddenly felt very sad.

"I don't think so," she said, shaking her head. "I'm just not ready for this, am I? I'm always going to make a mess of things."

"Stop feeling so sorry for yourself," urged Angie. "It can't do any harm, and it might even work!"

"I'm not even on the Internet, so it's pointless," hedged Tess.

"Doesn't matter," Angie told her. "You have an e-mail connection. I'll do the message but the guys will contact you direct on to your computer. Couldn't be simpler."

"OK," Tess agreed reluctantly. "But something tells me the whole stupid idea is just bound to blow up in my face."

* * *

The following week Tess sat at her desk gazing grimly at her computer screen. Angie was peering over her shoulder. She highlighted the ten answers she'd received so far. There were five proposals of marriage: two from students in Russia who thought it would be a good idea to come and live in England; two from a couple of lumberjacks in the northernmost tip of Newfoundland who explained that their part of the world was short of women and if she wanted to choose between them could she please bring a friend for the other; and one from a fur trapper in Greenland who kept a laptop computer in his log cabin but would far, far rather have a life partner there to keep him company.

"Yes, well, at least you're seeing the world," Angie said nervously. "You do get a few lonely people surfing the Web – it's natural."

"Doesn't seem natural to me," muttered Tess. "It's downright embarrassing. I knew this was a bad idea."

"Well, what about the other five?" Angie demanded. "Let's have a look." But these were no more inspiring than the first lot. There was a very severe woman from an

American university telling her that she was debasing herself by offering herself to men; three wedding accessory companies offering her excellent deals on invitation cards, flowers and cakes once her romance had reached its natural conclusion; and, finally, just as a crowning insult, a very verbose message from a poet in Tokyo who had read her description with great interest, was sure he was the right one for her, and would she please read his poetry and find him an English publisher.

"Oh, look – it's an attachment," remarked Angie. "Let's see what it says."

"You can if you think it's so fascinating!" muttered Tess, who had no intention of inspecting a library of Japanese poems, any more than she intended to make a note of cut-price confetti and discounted dinner menus. "Listen Angie, I want this to stop, now. I knew it was a bad idea and now we've proved it. So just cancel my message. Tell them I've left the country or something. This whole thing has got to finish now, OK?"

"OK, OK," Angie agreed good-naturedly. "It was worth a try, wasn't it? No harm done. Actually I think it was quite promising and if I wasn't getting on so well with Rod I might even give it a go myself."

After she'd disappeared Tess got down to some real work, much to the amazement of the rest of her office. She was so relieved to be back to normal after all those nightmare e-mails that she was almost enjoying the concerted effort.

About an hour later her screen flashed again, to tell her there was another e-mail. She clicked her mouse, almost dreading what she might find. Sure enough, it was another suitor – Angie obviously hadn't been able to stem the flow just yet. This time, the message was from a Ted in New York:

Hi from the Big Apple. I loved your message. I, too, am looking for a real, honest relationship where I don't have to pretend to be macho and tough. I am sick of meeting girls who claim to be sensitive and romantic but who don't allow men to be that way, always expecting us to be strong and dependable. Maybe it's because my job is in computers. Girls assume I am cold but I have a passionate soul and am looking for love. I have a really good feeling about you. And I adored the line at the end. Because more than anything I'm looking for a girl with a sense of humour. And if you're interested, I prefer soft centres.

For a while, Tess simply sat and stared at the message, hardly able to believe her eyes. Here he was – exactly the kind of guy she'd been looking for. It was as though he'd been conjured up by magic. There was just one little thing that bothered her.

"Angie!" she snapped into the telephone. "Just read me out that message you put on the Internet, would you?"

Obligingly, Angie read out the simple message, purporting to be from Tess, and saying she was looking for a man who was romantic and tender, not afraid to talk about his feelings, not afraid to have feelings...

"Yes, yes, yes," she said impatiently. "I know all that, it's exactly what we agreed. But what about the last line? How did it end?"

There was a slight pause before Angie replied. "Oh, that," she said awkwardly. "Yes, well, I improvised a bit there."

"What did you put?" demanded Tess through gritted teeth.

"Oh, I just added something you once said," Angie told her. "Some girls eat chocolate when they haven't got a boyfriend. Some girls prefer having chocolate to having a boyfriend. But I'm after a guy who will buy me chocolate – then make it unnecessary for me to eat any."

"Did I really say that," Tess asked suspiciously, hurriedly putting away a half-eaten Crunchie bar.

"Something like that," Angie said. "Don't you remember? It was when I got you that box of Black Magic for your birthday. I should have mentioned it, but I forgot. You don't mind, do you?"

"What?" Tess said distractedly. "Oh, er – no. No. That's fine. Thanks. Bye."

For the whole of the next month Tess felt as though she was starring in her own private movie – floating through delicious days and surfing through dreamy nights. Ted from New York contacted her almost every day. The more they corresponded the more intimate they became until it was as though this unseen, unheard man at the other end of a whole network of computers somehow had the key to her soul.

She came to work one morning after she and Angie had been to the cinema, still red-eyed from crying at the weepie bits. To her astonishment, the e-mail from Ted that afternoon said briefly:

Forgive me if I don't write a whole lot today. For some reason I'm feeling very sad. Are you quite happy, my angel, or is something making you unhappy, too? I don't know why, but there's a melancholy buzz in the air today.

How could he possibly have known, wondered Tess, that she'd been crying? It was amazing, even though she wasn't really sad, just moved by the film. After that, Tess found herself confiding more and more in Ted, telling him her innermost feelings. It was almost like writing a diary, she thought – certainly not like talking to a real-life boyfriend. Yet, increasingly, that was how Ted saw himself.

The more I get to know about you the more I like you. There's no pretence with you, no act that you have to put on to impress. When you write to me I know I'm hearing from the real Tess, my Tess...

* * *

"You're different, these days," Angie accused her, after the e-mail romance had been going for a couple of weeks. They were toying with sticky macaroni cheese in the staff canteen.

"How do you mean?" Tess wanted to know. But she didn't snap at Angie, as the old Tess might have done. She smiled and looked interested.

"Well, look at you," Angie went on. "You're getting too nice to be true. I don't like it one little bit. You keep smiling a soppy smile and not minding when people ask you stupid questions. If I didn't know you better I'd think you were, well, falling in love."

Tess smiled dreamily. "Maybe I am," she conceded.

Angie looked concerned. "Not with the e-mail guy?" she asked incredulously. "Listen, Tess – you can't be serious. I mean, I know that e-mail kick was my idea but it was a bit of fun. I never expected you to take it this seriously. You've never met the guy, right?"

"Maybe not in person – but I've met him all right," Tess said serenely.

"You don't know what he looks like, what he sounds like." Angie took a deep breath, summoning all her reasoning powers. "You don't know what he feels like. What if he has a wet handshake?"

"I don't care," Tess answered. "That's not important."

"What if he does those wet, sloppy kisses?" Angie persisted.

"He won't," Tess told her. "Anyway, it wouldn't matter. It's him that matters – him and me. The way we connect together. Do you know, he likes all the same movies as me, all the same books. He's a vegetarian, just like I am. It's uncanny – like meeting your other half."

"You're a hopeless case," concluded Angie, shaking her head in disbelief. "And I'm worried for you. Tess, if you carry on like this you're going to get hurt."

Tess smiled. "No, I'm not. That's the whole point. Angie, for the first time ever I've found someone I can confide in, someone I trust. It's making me look at the whole world differently."

"Hi, mind if I join you?" Dominic had arrived and was putting down his tray of food at their table.

Tess smiled at him, while Angie stared at her in open-mouthed amazement. Only a few weeks ago she'd have found some stinging retort to send him on his way. She certainly wouldn't have smiled at him and made room for him at the table.

"Great," Dominic went on. "You're looking really good at the moment, Tess, what are you taking?"

Angie held her breath. This was just the kind of remark that would normally incite Tess to one of her more flaming outbursts. But it didn't happen. She just shrugged and said: "Nothing special. What have you been up to lately, anyhow?"

While Angie fretted about the change in her friend, and Dominic rejoiced in it, Tess found herself drawn deeper and deeper into her flourishing new relationship. Ted was loving, intimate, tender – everything she'd always wanted in a man.

One day, we'll meet – really meet properly. I can't wait to meet you, hold you, get to know how you sound and look and feel...

There was just one thing that didn't quite add up. Ted never mentioned exactly where he lived. He seemed happy to communicate by e-mail. He didn't volunteer any other address, not even a telephone number. He said he wanted to see Tess and meet her, but he never asked for a photograph, nor offered to send one of himself.

"There you are," said Angie triumphantly, when Tess mentioned the mystery. "He's obviously hideous. You are having an affair with the ugliest man in America – and you don't even know it."

"I don't care," Tess replied, annoyingly. "It's what's inside that counts. That's the mistake I've been making all this time. I haven't bothered to look beyond the physical, to the person's true nature."

"Yeah, well, that's easy to say when the person's across the Atlantic Ocean with no mailing address," Angie couldn't help saying. "If he was actually here, right now, you'd care about what he looked like all right."

"Do you mean, that's what you care about – with Rod?" Tess asked. Ever since the Valentine Disco, Angie and Rod had been going out together.

Angie blushed. "Partly," she confessed. "Look, we get on fine. I really like him and everything. But I can't separate that from liking his face, and the way he smiles. And the way he kisses. Especially the way he kisses…"

It was about a month after that first message from Ted, that Tess's boss Marion called her into her office. "Ah, Tess dear," she said kindly. "I have a little request. I've been asked to speak at an international conference – it's all about how to communicate public policy. Apparently only three local government press offices have been asked, so it's quite an honour."

Marion blushed girlishly, obviously very pleased. Tess smiled at her affectionately. The old stick wasn't so bad, she thought kindly. In fact, she was pretty good at her job, and she deserved to be noticed. "Congratulations," Tess said warmly. "You'll be brilliant."

Marion hesitated. "Yes, well, that's not quite all, Tess. You see, there are all kinds of important sessions at this conference. I may have to attend several different ones on different subjects. What I'd really like is someone to come with me to make sure I have all the notes and briefings I need. Someone who can cope with all the new technology. I've noticed how brilliantly you've been progressing with your own computer lately."

Tess glanced up, alarmed, wondering whether Marion had noticed all the time she spent locked into her e-mail routine. But Marion wasn't being sarcastic. "So I'd very much like you to accompany me," she went on. "All expenses paid, of course. The conference has offered me that facility…"

"I'd love to," Tess said at once. "Er – where is the conference?"

"Oh, didn't I mention that?" said Marion vaguely, rifling through some papers on her desk. "Ah, yes – here it is. It's in New York…"

Tess left Marion's office, her heart singing wildly. New York, New York! The song pattered through her brain all day. At last she'd be able to meet Ted, to see him. Her on-screen lover would finally become real.

Excitedly she dashed off a message to Ted, telling him she was coming to New York, enthusing about how wonderful it would be to meet him at last, overflowing with love and confidence and high expectation.

So she was very surprised when nothing came back. Nothing at all. She waited half an hour, then an hour. Still no message. Perhaps hers had somehow got lost. So she sent it again. There was still no reply.

The next day she dashed eagerly to work, convinced that Ted would have sent her a message overnight. But there was nothing all day.

That evening, Tess trudged home and went straight to her room. She lay face down on the bed, turned on the saddest music she could find, and began to weep copious, miserable tears. The little bubble of hope and happiness that had been growing day by day, ever since that first message from Ted, had burst, leaving her more desolate and alone than she had ever felt before.

Oh, sure, she'd been upset that evening when Gavin had treated her so badly. But she'd hardly known him – she'd just fallen for the idea of him and hadn't liked it when he hadn't lived up to her expectations. What she'd felt then had been nothing – nothing, compared with the heartbreak that tormented her now.

Ted had been her one chance of a decent relationship – a romance she couldn't spoil with her sharp tongue and quick, nervous retorts. Somehow, being able to write to him had unleashed something inside her – a softer, sweeter, more loving Tess. But it was a more vulnerable Tess, too. She was feeling so hurt, so rejected, so utterly wretched – and all because she'd allowed herself to feel something real.

Sobbing uncontrollably, she punched a couple of times at her pillow. It was better before, she thought angrily. Sure, she'd been unkind and uncaring, sure she'd hurt people and trampled on their feelings. But that had to be better than this terrible sense of betrayal and misery that was assaulting her now that she'd let her defences down and let someone see her true self.

All evening Tess stayed locked in her room. She wouldn't talk to anyone, wouldn't even come down for supper. Her worried mother banged on the door. "Tess, Tess, are you OK?"

"Fine," she called in a frail, weary voice. Then she just lay in the darkness, listening to the rain beating against the window, until at last she fell into a troubled sleep.

"Tess, what's happened?" Angie demanded the next day, when they met as usual in the canteen. "You're looking dreadful."

"Oh, nothing," said poor Tess bitterly. "It's just that you were right, as usual, and

I was wrong." She explained how Ted had cut off all communication the minute she'd announced that she was coming to New York. "So, you see, I have got hurt, just as you said I would. I wish we'd never started this whole thing."

Angie listened sympathetically, then shook her head and sighed. "There you go again," she commented. "Jumping to conclusions as usual. First you fall in love with the guy, even though you've never seen him. Then, the minute there's the tiniest little hitch, you go playing the drama queen and deciding it's all over and time to kill yourself."

"Well, you have to admit the prospects of a happy ending are pretty slim," reasoned Tess.

"Rubbish," responded sensible, down-to-earth Angie. "There could be all kinds of explanations. He could be ill."

Tess looked alarmed. "Oh no – I never thought of that. Oh, my poor, poor boy. Suppose he's been in an accident. Suppose he's in hospital. Suppose he's all by himself and no one knows he's cut his foot with the bread knife and can't get to the phone..."

"You're doing it again, Tess," Angie

reminded her, drumming her fingers on the table. "Just listen to me. I said it was a possibility, that's all. Or he could have been called out of town. Or – I know – they're always having power cuts in New York, aren't they? Maybe he's been cut off and has to reload his computer. All I'm saying is, give the guy a chance, Tess. Don't assume the worst."

Tess grinned at her. "You're right," she said, her face brightening. "Maybe everything will work out after all."

As soon as she got to her desk, she fired off another message to Ted, then tried to bury herself in her work. But it was impossible. Every few minutes she found herself tapping the familiar keys that took her back to the e-mail option. And every time, she was disappointed. By late afternoon – morning in America – Tess was frantic.

She called Computer Services, her voice squeaking with agitation. "My whole system is breaking down!" she yelled, almost back to her old, stinging self. "Get me Barry and tell him it's urgent!"

Barry appeared half an hour later, looking even more unkempt than usual, his shirt only half tucked into his trousers, his hair unruly, his brow furrowed. Normally Barry could be relied on to be calm and even-tempered, but now there was something wild about him, something almost nervous.

At first, though, Tess was too distracted to notice. "My e-mails aren't working," she announced, without even saying hello. "This whole system is rubbish, if you ask me. Will you just put me back on-line, boot me up, jack me in, log me up – whatever…"

Barry took her place at the computer and tapped a few keys concentratedly. He frowned, then turned to her. "I'm sorry, Tess. There isn't anything wrong with your computer," he said quietly. Too quietly.

"Yes, there is," Tess retorted. "There has to be." Even as she spoke, her heart was sinking. Barry was right, she told herself. There was nothing wrong with the computer. Ted simply wasn't going to reply to this e-mail any more than any of the others. He hadn't replied – because he hadn't wanted to. All the happiness, trust, confidence, even the love she had begun to feel – it all rested, she saw suddenly, on this one device. If the computer was broken, Ted still loved her. If it wasn't – he had betrayed her, drawn her into a love affair and then dropped her without even a word. And without an address or a phone number, she'd never, ever, find out why.

No, she told herself. Barry had to be wrong. He just had to be. "Have another look," she urged him desperately. "Maybe it's just my external connection. Come to think of it, that must be it. I've been getting internal memos OK, but nothing from outside. Don't you think that's it, Barry?"

Barry gave her a long, steady look, then shook his head. Tess eyed him wildly, furious at his refusal to accept her suggestion. "Tess," he said with a sigh. "There's something I've been meaning to tell you."

"I don't care what you've got to tell me!" stormed Tess. "Don't you understand? My whole life is falling apart and you're not even helping me."

Barry just carried on staring at her, his deep blue eyes unblinking behind his thick glasses. "Tess, you'd better hear me out," he said softly. A message flashed on to the screen.

"Quick!" Tess screeched. "You see? You must've done something. Look! It's from him! I know it is!"

118

Sure enough, up came the familiar code, signalling that the message was from Ted in New York. Tess's heart began to soar. Then she looked puzzled. The message was unlike anything Ted had ever written before. It was starkly practical:

Please read enclosure.

Tess practically pulled Barry out of the way so that she could sit at her screen. "Oh, no!" she wailed. "Ted's never sent an enclosure before. Now, how do I do that thing? It's the launch button or something, right?"

Silently, Barry watched as her trembling hand guided the mouse over the icon, clicked, and waited. Both of them stared at the screen. Then, to her amazement, a lavish, full-colour picture began to etch itself into view. It was the forest – the forest of that Valentine's message. There were the trees and shrubs, the squirrel and the bee. There, suddenly, were the two lovebirds. Only this time, one of them came flying to the centre of the screen and stood perched on a branch as a caption formed beneath it.

I love you. Barry.

Tess stared at the picture, stared at Barry's pale, tense face, then back at the picture again. "I – I don't get it," she faltered. "How could Ted have sent me the Valentine, when we'd never even met? And if this is from him – how come you've put your own message on it? And your message ... what does it mean?"

"It means what it says," Barry told her quietly. "And it probably means you're going to hate me for it. But listen, Tess. You have to give me a chance."

Slowly, Tess turned to him, her eyes fixed on his. She was too confused to do anything but listen.

"First of all, there is no Ted," Barry told her heavily.

Tess gasped. "You mean...?"

Barry nodded. "He doesn't exist. I'm sorry, Tess – I shouldn't have done it, I know. But once it had started, once you began to confide in me, once I got to know the real Tess ... I just couldn't stop. I fell in love, and the more I fell in love, the more I knew that what I was doing was bound to make you hate me."

"So it was you all along," Tess murmured, stunned. "You sent the Valentine. And then you replied to that Internet message?"

Barry nodded again, looking even more

uncomfortable. "You see, that evening at the Valentine's disco, I overheard you and Angie planning to post up a message on the Loveline Bulletin. So I decided this was my chance to get to know you."

"But why did you pretend to be Ted from New York?" Tess asked, after a long, stunned pause.

Barry shrugged. "Oh, because I wanted to be anonymous and glamorous. Glamorous so that you'd be interested enough to reply to me. Anonymous so that you could be yourself without having to put on an image or pretend to be something you're not."

"That doesn't reflect very well on me," said Tess rather quietly. "But I guess I deserve it. I've never been very nice to you, have I?"

Barry shrugged. "Not exactly, no. But you've always interested me, Tess, ever since you first dragged me up here to shout at me because you couldn't get the hang of your damned computer. You're funny and bright and there's something different about you. I just wanted us to have the chance to get to know each other properly."

"Well, you've certainly got to know me," Tess said, blushing as she remembered all those messages detailing her most intimate thoughts and feelings.

"Yes, and it's – it's been a revelation," Barry muttered. "Like you said on the e-mail – once you're in love, that's it. Everything you discover about the person just makes you love them more."

"I didn't say that to you," Tess snapped. "It was to Ted. How was I to know he didn't even exist? That my nice, romantic American had been usurped by – by…" But she didn't finish her sentence. Barry was looking at her so intensely. Somehow, those eyes of his, hidden behind the thick glasses, looked different all of a sudden – they were a piercing blue, Tess realized. And they were smouldering.

"I don't suppose you'll ever want to talk to me after this," he said sadly. "But I want you to know it was all true. All of it. I do cry at sentimental movies. I am a vegetarian. I do care about the girl inside you – very much. Even though I quite like the way you look as well. I meant everything. I still mean it. I'm just sorry it happened this way, and sorry if I caused you any pain."

His voice was shaking as he got up to leave. There was a hushed silence from everyone else, who had been staring over their desks at the curious encounter being played out before them.

Tess got up and glared at them. "What are you lot all staring at?" she demanded, then raced out of the office and down the corridor to the lift.

Barry had just stepped inside and the doors were closing when Tess caught up with him, and began wildly pressing buttons, hammering on the doors, yelling for him to wait for her. The doors opened, she stepped in, and then there were just the two of them, riding up to the very top of the building.

Barry looked at her questioningly, hardly daring to hope. Tess smiled at him.

"OK – you win," she said almost shyly. "If it's been you I've been getting to know all these weeks – then it's you I want to be with."

"Really?" said Barry, pushing back his glasses which, as usual, were sliding down his nose. "Really?" Tess nodded, Barry pressed "B" for basement, and as the lift made its slow descent down the full length of the building, he bent his head to hers.

His lips were full and soft and sensual, his embrace warm and loving. Tess closed her eyes. At last, she was in the arms of the mysterious sender of all those messages of love and tenderness. At last she knew what it was like to feel him, touch him, kiss him. And, with a sudden rush of happiness, she understood what it was she was feeling: it was like coming home after a long, long time in the wilderness.

Too Far to Go

Alison Creaghan

It was a perfect day. Silver clouds scudded across the blue, late summer sky as Colin and Jessica walked, hand in hand, in the woods near Colin's home. His parents were on holiday so when they got back the two of them had the house to themselves. They ate sliced tomato and salami on wholemeal bread for lunch, then sat out in the sun.

Colin and Jessica had been together for the best part of three years, since their first term at sixth-form college. And Colin had been crazy about Jessica since they shared a fourth-form class at secondary school. Back in those days, Colin was the kind of boy who spent too much time alone with his computer. He didn't know how to talk to a girl.

Jessica was small, with straight blonde hair and an intense gaze which frightened some people off. She wore round glasses and had no figure at all. Boys didn't interest her. The only thing Jessica seemed to care about was being the cleverest girl in the class. Colin used to fantasize about her taking off his glasses, then him taking off hers. At that point, the two of them would suddenly see each other, as if for the first time. Somehow, they would end up kissing.

In the real world it was two years before they had their first kiss. By then, Jessica had filled out and taken to wearing contact lenses. Colin was less shy. He'd started taking care over how he dressed and wore his hair. Even so, he seemed to have left it too late. Loads of boys were already after Jessica. Colin thought he had no chance.

He was wrong. One night, at a party, he'd asked her to dance and Jessica had fallen into his arms. Their friends agreed that they were made for each other. They seemed to make a perfect couple.

But nothing stays perfect for ever. As they dozed in the sun, the sky began to cloud over and the clouds started to turn dark. Summer was nearly over. Soon, all their problems would begin again.

Two summers before, it had all seemed so easy. They'd each applied to the same universities, for the same courses – media degrees with a heavy practical element, which were in short supply. Southampton offered Jessica a place, but turned Colin down. Durham had a course which Colin was accepted for, but they weren't impressed by Jessica's GCSE grades, and didn't even give her an interview.

The two of them talked about taking a year out, applying to different places, but both knew that they'd be mad to turn down the chances they already had. It was only for three years, they told themselves. At the end of it, they'd both get jobs in London, move in together.

But three years was a long time, and the last one hadn't been easy. They were both enjoying their courses, but neither of them was too good at making friends. Jessica had had the same two best friends since primary school, while Colin had always been a loner. During that first year, they'd missed each other terribly.

"What are you thinking?" Jessica asked, when they'd moved inside from the cold.

"Oh, just ... how we're going to manage for another two years, now that I've got used to you being around all the time again." Jessica squeezed his thigh.

"I was thinking the same thing," she said.

Something about the way she said it made him feel uncomfortable.

"And...?" he asked

"Oh, nothing. It doesn't get any easier, does it?"

That evening, they went to eat at Jessica's house. Afterwards, Colin helped her dad to wash up.

"Two weeks to go," Mr Ross said. "Will you be glad to get out of here?"

"Not me," Colin told him. "I like it here."

"Think you'll come back after you've finished university?"

"I doubt it. We were thinking more of London. That's where all the jobs are."

"We?"

Colin shut up. He never knew how much Jessica told people about their plans.

"I was trying to persuade Jessica to consider doing an MA in the States," Mr Ross revealed. "It's where the real media opportunities are. But that's a long way off yet."

Colin wondered why Jessica hadn't mentioned this idea to him.

"I've been meaning to say," Jessica told him the next day as he was driving her home from the Savoy after a mediocre movie, "when we're back at uni, I think we should – you know – go out more with other people."

Colin swerved in the road, and narrowly avoided smashing his mum's car into a pedestrian refuge.

"What do you mean?" he asked, slowing down.

"It just seems like – whenever I visit you – you haven't made many friends."

Colin protested. "That's because when you come I want to spend all my time with you. I can see other people as much as I like at other times."

Colin wished he saw more of Jessica during term time. Westtown, where they both lived, was about halfway between Southampton and Durham. Durham was a three-hour drive, Southampton more like four. They could meet at home for the weekend, but had only managed to visit each other at university twice. The train journey between Durham and Southampton took well over five hours if you went through London (there were five changes if you went the cheaper, cross-country way). Even with a railcard, the ticket cost a fortune. It was too far to go.

"So you do have friends you haven't told me about?" Jessica asked, gently.

"Sure, I … uh…"

The truth was, Colin didn't have that many friends. But if he got lonely he could always call Jessica.

"Do you know any girls at all?"

Girls? Where did girls come into it?

"Girls? There are some on my corridor. What are you getting at?"

"Do you ever go out with any of them?"

"Of course not," Colin protested, finding it hard to keep his eyes on the road. "I'm going out with you."

"But I'm not in Durham," Jessica said. "I wouldn't mind you seeing other girls, not at all."

Slowly, the penny began to drop.

"Do you see other boys?" Colin asked, in a quiet voice.

"All the time," Jessica said. "I know loads of boys. You've met most of them."

She had introduced him to various lads in the hall of residence where she lived. Colin couldn't remember their names. He had tried to forget their faces, worried that one day he and Jessica would have the very conversation that they were having today.

Colin asked the question he dreaded the answer to.

"And do you ... *go out* with any of them?"

Why was she telling him this now, just before they went back? Why hadn't they had this out at the beginning of the holiday?

"I've been out with three or four different boys."

"Who?"

He felt like he was choking.

"Jerry, Mike, Peter, Carl. I've mentioned them all to you."

"Not that you *went out* with them."

Jessica's voice went high pitched, the way it did when she was starting to get upset.

"Went out doesn't mean slept with, Colin. And I did mention it, but you didn't seem to register what I was trying to tell you."

"What did you do with them?" Colin asked, in a sullen voice.

"Went to a film, or a play, or a party ... what does it matter?"

"I meant ... what did you *do* with them?"

"They got a peck on the cheek at the end of the evening, if that's what you're asking. I'm not telling you this because I'm feeling guilty."

"Why are you telling me, then? Why haven't you told me before?"

"Because I was worried you'd be jealous."

She was right to worry. Colin couldn't bear the thought of losing Jessica.

"Nothing happened, Colin," Jessica insisted, as he pulled up outside her door and turned off the engine.

"I want to spend the rest of my life with you," he whispered.

"I feel the same way," Jessica said. "But I don't want to be the only woman who you've ever been friendly with."

"That's silly."

"Is it?"

Colin was an only child. He wasn't used to a lot of female company. When he had to work with women on his course, he got on well with them, but he didn't make much effort to mix socially. He'd feel disloyal to Jessica if he did.

"Coming in?" she asked him.

He shook his head. "I want to think about a few things."

Colin drove off, into the countryside, his head burning up with thoughts of Jessica going out with other boys. He didn't get home for a long time.

*   *   *

"Did you tell him?" Jessica's mum asked when she got inside.

"Kind of."

"How did he take it?"

"Not too well," Jessica told her mother. "He wouldn't come in."

She'd talked through what she was going to say with Mum the night before. Jessica hadn't enjoyed the film, worrying it over in her head.

It wasn't that she wanted to finish with Colin. She loved him. There'd been no one before him and, probably, there'd be no one after. Yet, all this summer, she'd been worried that their relationship was starting to stagnate. It felt like they had the whole thing on hold until they'd finished university. They were nineteen years old. They couldn't live their lives like that.

Colin talked about how they'd live together in London, but it all seemed so far away. Colin wanted to be a documentary maker. He wanted to work for the BBC or Channel 4. Jessica used to say that she wanted to do something similar, but was no longer sure what she wanted. The longer she was away from home, the less certain she was about anything.

Before they ended up going to different universities, she and Colin had planned to get work experience in their summer holidays – something they could put on their CVs when they were applying for jobs. But that had been too complicated to arrange when they were living far apart, so they'd both come home.

The trouble was that, after being at university, home was boring. There was nothing going on. Lots of her friends were away, so Jessica was short of female company. Colin said all that mattered was their seeing each other. Jessica wasn't so sure. She loved Colin. She couldn't see herself marrying anyone other than Colin, who suited her like an old, comfortable slipper, who was clever and considerate and doted on her.

Doted. That was part of the problem. Maybe Colin loved her too much. Jessica needed to see other people, needed to get things in perspective. Her whole life couldn't be held in check by a promise she'd made when she was seventeen. Life would have been so much easier if they'd both managed to go to the same university.

Or would it? Jessica wondered. If they'd been able to see each other as much as they wanted: doing the same course during the day, socializing at night, hardly meeting anyone else, would they have lasted the year?

She didn't know.

The last few days of the holiday drifted by. Colin didn't mention the conversation they'd had in the car that night, and neither did Jessica. She'd said what she needed to say and couldn't bear to go over it all again. Whatever happened would be whatever happened.

On their last night before returning to university, Jessica and Colin were alone in her bedroom. Mum and Dad were out for the evening. They wouldn't be disturbed. Jessica had been to have her hair done, shortening and shaping it into a straight blonde bob. Colin said he liked it, though Jessica suspected he was only being polite. His own hair, once long, was now neatly styled to the nape of his neck. He had filled out a little over the last year and was no longer so lanky. He had never looked better, Jessica thought. She'd been mad to think of finishing with him. She couldn't imagine loving anyone more than she loved Colin.

"I want to ask you something," Colin said.

"What?"

Jessica was expecting him to ask when he could next come down to visit her in Southampton. She would ask him to wait until she knew her schedule for the term. But instead, he said:

"Why don't we get engaged?"

"You mean, as in *engaged to be married*?"

"Yes. Not set a date or anything but..."

Jessica couldn't stop blinking. Her contact lenses had suddenly become very dry.

"I don't know what to say," she said.

"Say yes. We could go into town tomorrow, choose a ring."

Jessica was nonplussed. She wasn't sure that she believed in marriage, or being *engaged*. People like her didn't do things like that. She tried to explain her feelings to Colin, but the words all came out wrong.

"It's not that I don't ... I wouldn't want you to spend your money on ... we're too young to..."

"It was only an idea," Colin said, backtracking rapidly. He looked upset.

"Is this because of what I said about

seeing other people?" Jessica asked, her voice almost a whisper. He mumbled, too embarrassed to look her in the eyes.

"Sort of."

"I love you, Colin. There's no need to try and tie me down."

He ought to realize that, if anything, trying to tie her down would have the opposite effect.

"Let's change the subject," Colin said.

"I don't want to change the subject," Jessica told him. "I don't want us to hide from things."

"You want me to see other people," Colin argued. "But I don't."

"Don't then. All I meant was..."

"I know what you meant."

Jessica didn't want to leave it this way, to have a row on their last night.

"I'm not trying to finish with you," she said, tears forming in the corners of her eyes. "I'm trying to find a way for us to stay together, but keep growing. Don't you s e?"

And then it was Colin who was crying, and they were holding on to each other, and hugging, and everything was all right.

For a while.

*   *   *

"Do you think you could show me how to adjust this?"

The girl with the crew cut kept losing half a second on her edit. Colin understood the problem. He used to fix this kind of equipment all the time back at secondary school.

"You've probably got the settings wrong," he said. "I'll take a look." The realignment took him two seconds.

"Thanks," Crew Cut said. "Can I ask you something else?" She must be a first year. He hadn't seen her around before. Colin didn't generally like short hair on girls, but this girl's close crop suited her better than Jessica's new look.

"What?" Colin said.

"I'm in a band." She had a Geordie accent, so she must be local. "Do you think I could get away with using the equipment here to make us a promo video?"

"No problem," Colin said, "as long as you don't pick the busiest times. But you won't get very far with what you're using now. You need special software to synchronize the music."

"Oh." She looked so disappointed that

Colin heard himself say, "I might know where to get hold of it."

Colin had helped some friends make early videos for their band, the Blacks, who were doing all right now, he explained. He could probably borrow some software from them.

"That'd be brilliant. We're doing a gig in Newcastle next weekend. Would you like to come, meet the rest of the group?"

"Er, maybe. I might be visiting my girl-friend. Can I let you know?" He thought he saw a flicker of disappointment when he mentioned his girlfriend.

"I'll tell you what," she said. "I'll put your name on the guest list anyway. Plus one. What do they call you?"

"Colin. Colin Kane."

She gave him the details of the gig.

"I'm Sandy, but my stage name's Newt. Hope you can make it, Colin."

Colin hoped he wouldn't be able to. Jessica kept putting him off. She had an assignment to finish, or there was a film she was helping with and they had to work every weekend. Colin offered to help, too. No dice.

Jessica did turn out to be busy. Colin hadn't given Newt's band another thought, but then it was Saturday night and, as usual, he had nothing much to do. How could it hurt to go along?

The club was small and there were only about thirty people in the audience. The group were called Pond Life. Their music was poppier than Colin liked. Newt, the lead singer, had a good voice but moved jerkily, like an insect. He could see why she'd been given her silly stage name. It was an arresting image but didn't seem to fit with the music the group played. Sandy wasn't attractive, Colin decided, not in a conventional sense. But she had something.

Afterwards, Newt introduced him to the rest of the band.

"Colin directed two videos for the Blacks," she boasted. The other Pond creatures were suitably impressed. They gave Colin a lift back to his halls in the band van.

"I stuck around here because I want to make a go of both my degree and the group," Newt explained. "Think I made the right decision?"

"Maybe."

"So, will you help us make a video?"

"Why not?"

Before they'd dropped him off, he'd agreed

to spend the next weekend shooting the video and the following one editing it.

Of course, those turned out to be the only two weekends all term that Jessica decided he could come and visit her.

"I suppose I could reschedule," Colin offered.

"No. Don't do that," Jessica said. "It's good that you're..."

"I don't want to make rock videos," Colin reminded her. "I still want to make documentaries. It's just that this girl from my course..."

"Really. I'm fine with it," Jessica told him. "And music videos might help you to get a job. I should think about doing one myself."

"You could come and help," Colin offered.

"It's OK," Jessica said. "Not long till Christmas, after all."

"I'm not going out with this girl," Colin over-explained. "I don't even fancy her."

"Don't you understand, Colin?" Jessica asked. "It's all right if you do fancy her. You're not a monk."

She rang off, giving Colin a sleepless night.

Jessica didn't want to fall in love. She went out with Daniel a couple of times because of the film he was working on, his final year project, that was all. She was picking up experience by working as his script editor. In the long run, Jessica still wanted to work on factual programmes, but some drama experience couldn't hurt.

What happened next was that Daniel suggested that she looked perfect for a bit part in his film, playing a reporter. Naturally, Jessica was flattered. But that was the point at which she made it clear to Daniel that she had a boyfriend, just in case he was encouraging her for the wrong reasons.

"I don't know where you find the time," was all Daniel said in response.

Daniel was a gorgeous, gentle Irishman. Half the girls on the course had fantasies about him. Even so, Jessica got the feeling that he was interested in her. During the weeks that the team were working on the film, however, Daniel didn't put a word (or a hand) out of place. Jessica felt almost insulted. At sixth-form college, where everybody knew that she was going out with Colin, boys usually left her alone. But at university, she'd got used to having plenty of attention. It was both flattering and comforting. For the first few years of her teens, Jessica had believed that boys were hopelessly intimidated by clever girls.

They finished shooting the film. Daniel still hadn't tried it on. Jessica felt guilty for thinking about him all the time. Half-heartedly, she tried to arrange to see Colin, but was relieved when he turned out to be too busy. *This is just a crush,* she told herself. *I'll get over it.* When she'd talked to Colin about seeing other boys, Jessica wasn't expecting something like this to happen. She didn't know what she'd been expecting. Now that it was happening, Jessica felt lost. It wasn't Colin she was worried about, Jessica realized, guiltily: it was herself. She couldn't stand it if Daniel didn't care.

The next Saturday night, Jessica went to the university film club on her own. Most of her friends had dates. There were no parties on and, anyway, she wanted to watch Fellini's *La Dolce Vita*, to see what all the fuss was about.

"Mind if I join you?"

Daniel was standing in the queue behind her. He, too, was alone.

"Be my guest."

"I've missed working with you," he said, blue eyes twinkling.

"Me too."

He brushed the curly hair out of his eyes and added, "No boyfriend this weekend?"

"No boyfriend all term. He's at Durham. It's a long way to come."

Daniel nodded. "I tried to hang on to my girlfriend back home for two years."

"Two years?"

"I was mad about her. We'd been together from when I was seventeen and she was fifteen. Then, in the summer, she told me that she'd been seeing my best friend since Christmas."

"How awful."

"I'm not looking forward to going home much."

"Me neither," Jessica heard herself say, and hoped that Daniel didn't ask her to explain why.

After the film, Daniel walked Jessica back to her room, and stayed for coffee. Still, he didn't do anything. Daniel wouldn't do to Colin what his best friend had done to him. Jessica felt awful for wishing that he would.

"Can we do this again?" he asked, shaking her hand goodnight.

"I'd love to," she told him, and made a date to meet the next weekend.

Colin must be mad. How come he had turned down the chance to see Jessica in order to make a poxy band video? Actually, the shoot had gone quite well. Newt, with her crew cut and sharp features, looked surprisingly good on the small screen. During the week, Colin worked late into the night, forsaking sleep to edit the video and give himself a clear weekend. Newt kept coming along to the editing suite, bringing him coffee and cakes to keep him going. They had a good laugh together. On Wednesday night, Colin asked her a favour.

"Do you think that I could borrow the band van for the weekend? I'd like to drive to Southampton and see my girlfriend, surprise her."

"I'll ask," she promised, with disappointment in her eyes.

Next night, she said he could. She even brought the van over on Friday and showed him how to cope with the gearbox.

"I really appreciate it," Colin told Newt.

"It's the least we could do," she told him. "After what you've done for us. The video's looking brilliant. I just hope that your girlfriend appreciates what she's got in you."

Colin smiled. Jessica had never been very interested in his rock video work. Nevertheless, he took a copy of the rough cut to show her.

Colin set off at four on Friday and only made brief break stops along the way, but it was getting on for midnight when he parked outside Jessica's hall of residence. He put the van in a loading zone, hoping that vigilant porters wouldn't clamp it in the morning.

Jessica had a new room this year, and it took him a while to work out where to find her. Then he had to sort out the hall security system. When he got to Jessica's corridor, Colin began to worry. Suppose she wasn't there? She might be at a party or worse, with another guy. But he could hear music coming from inside the room. Colin was about to knock when he heard Jessica's door begin to open. He took a few steps back.

"Wait," Jessica's voice said, as the song ended.

A handsome, curly haired boy leant back

into the room. Colin saw the edge of Jessica's body, in a brown dress he knew well.

"See you tomorrow night," she said.

"I can't wait," a lilting Irish accent replied.

The well-built boy headed off in the opposite direction from Colin, leather jacket swung over his shoulders.

Colin stood in the hallway, wondering what to do. He couldn't go back to Durham tonight. He was too tired. He could sleep in the back of the van, but it was very cold out. He might get hypothermia. Could he confront Jessica? To make a scene would be so embarrassing, so awful ... but, if he didn't, he might lose her. And, anyway, it was possible that he'd arrived just in time, before things got really serious. He could stop it now... Colin stood in the hall as music continued to play from her room, masking the sound of his heart breaking.

Jessica felt both giddy and guilty. She'd had a brilliant evening with Daniel, talking about everything under the sun. But he'd never have done anything if she hadn't started it. She'd pulled him towards her as he tried to shake her hand goodnight. Then she'd given him a short but satisfying kiss. Would Daniel think that she was loose, kissing him like that when he knew that she already had a boyfriend?

Jessica did feel bad about it. But Colin was so far away. She got lonely. And Daniel was so different from him. The world in which she was falling for Daniel was so different from the world in which she loved Colin. Maybe she could keep the two worlds apart.

There was a knock on her door. Jessica looked around, trying to see what Daniel had left behind. Nothing. Maybe he was going to tell her that he couldn't bring himself to leave, that he had to stay with her tonight, otherwise he would... *Stop fantasizing!* she told herself, and opened the door.

"I hope you're not disappointed," Colin said.

He had the look on his face which showed that he was suppressing anger. He'd seen something, she was sure. Jessica hesitated a second too long before embracing him.

"You nearly caught me with another man," she said, in a jokey, not quite convincing, voice. "The bloke whose film I've been working on. He just left."

Colin sighed with relief. She'd taken the wind from his sails.

"I'm glad I didn't interrupt anything," he commented, sounding cynical. "I know I should have warned you I was coming, but I only got to borrow the van at short notice."

"Don't be daft," Jessica told him. "It's wonderful to see you."

The following night, Daniel was giving a showing of his final year film.

"This is Colin, my boyfriend," Jessica told him, in the viewing room.

"I've heard a lot about you," Daniel said, shaking Colin's hand. "It sounds like we have a lot of interests in common."

"So I believe," Colin told him. "I'm looking forward to your film."

There was a gang of Daniel's friends and a handful of his lecturers at the première. This was what Jessica had meant about tomorrow night, Colin realized. It wasn't as bad as he'd feared.

Colin wanted to dislike the film, but it was actually pretty good. The story wasn't too original but the dialogue was crisp and

Jessica was a revelation. Colin had never seen her act before. When she'd told him about the role, he'd assumed that she was playing a sexy part, showing her legs a lot. But no. She wore her old glasses and played a frustrated, silly woman who was too stupid a reporter to notice a murder committed under her nose.

"Neat comedy," Colin told Daniel afterwards.

"Thanks. It wouldn't have been half so good without Jessica's help."

"Who are you going to show it to? Someone who'll give you a job next year?"

One good thing about Daniel, Colin thought, he was a third year. In a few months he'd be gone.

"Actually," the boy told him, "that bloke over there is from the Southampton School of Film and Television. I'm hoping that they're going to give me a place on their one-year course."

From the way that the guy came over, all smiles and superlatives, Colin was pretty sure that he would. Inside, he was beginning to get angry, but Daniel was giving him no excuse to behave badly. He seemed rather likeable. Maybe Jessica had been telling him the truth last night. She'd said that she and Daniel were only interested in each other as friends.

"Didn't you bring a video?" Jessica asked, when most people had gone.

"Yes, but..."

"Oh, Colin. Please put it on."

It was the last thing Colin wanted to do, but he could hardly refuse in front of Daniel. It would make him look small, scared to compete.

"All right," he said.

Daniel got out a videoplayer, hooked it up to the projector, and they put the video on.

"It's only a rough cut," Colin warned as the timecode appeared on the screen.

He was pleased to see his work blown up to cinema size, but couldn't work up much enthusiasm for the film. He was fed up with the images and the song.

"Striking-looking lead singer," Daniel said, as it finished. "What's she called?"

"Newt."

"Mind if we play it again?"

"Yes, go on," Jessica insisted.

This time, everyone agreed that the song was growing on them.

"I like the story, too," Daniel said. "I didn't

get it the first time – the images were too arresting – but that's the way it should be with rock videos. They repay repeated viewing."

"Thanks," Colin said. "Actually, I liked the way in your film you seemed to be using a flashback, but it turned out to be the future. It had me fooled."

The two men talked film for nearly an hour, leaving everyone else out of the conversation. By now, Colin couldn't help it. He liked Daniel a lot. He could see what Jessica saw in him. He ought to be jealous. But Colin was the one who Jessica took back to her room that night. What did Colin have to be jealous about?

He returned the van to Newt late on Sunday night, as he'd promised. Newt still lived with her parents in a village half way between Newcastle and Durham. She drove him back to his hall.

"Good weekend?" she asked.

"Brilliant. Everyone loved you in the video. They thought the song should be a hit."

"You showed them our video?" Newt exploded. "Before the rest of the band have seen it? How could you, Colin Kane?"

Newt stopped the van half a mile from

halls and made him walk the rest of the way. Colin couldn't understand why she was so upset.

"I like Colin. He's a nice guy."

"I know."

Jessica and Daniel had gone to see the new Woody Allen film. Now they were walking back to Daniel's place, arms linked casually, like close friends. Or that was how Jessica thought it looked. Despite Colin's visit last weekend, no sooner had he gone than he was out of her mind. Jessica felt awful, but couldn't help it. She was crazy about Daniel.

"I suppose," he said, as he made her a coffee, "that I should forget about that kiss you gave me last Friday night."

"I suppose..." Jessica repeated.

She was starting to cry. He sat down and put an arm around her.

"What is it?"

"I don't want to hurt Colin," she said.

"Neither do I."

Jessica wiped her eyes.

"I'm sorry," she said. "It's just that I have these feelings for you and I can't take them lightly. Maybe it would be better if I go."

Daniel only let her get as far as the door.

"I'd never forgive myself if I didn't tell you," he said. "It might be wrong but ... Jessica, I love you."

"I love you too," she whispered, tears forming in her eyes.

They kissed. This time, there was no turning back.

The letter came ten days after Colin had visited Jessica in Southampton. Colin already knew that something was wrong. Their two phone conversations since his visit had been both brief and vague. Jessica had sounded completely noncommittal.

The letter was short and to the point.

One day, it ended, *I hope that we can be friends again. Please get over me. You're a wonderful person. I'm sure that you'll find someone in Durham soon, as long as you give yourself half a chance.*

Jessica didn't go home that Christmas, preferring to visit Daniel in Dublin. Without her, Colin couldn't bring himself to visit their mutual friends. He had a miserable time. Life didn't seem worth living.

Back at university, Colin absorbed himself in work. There was always a bit more that he could do, always someone that he could help. At first, he hardly noticed that Newt wasn't around any more. She'd said something, he seemed to recall, about Pond Life doing a tour, missing a week or two of the course. When it got to February, he rang up her home to find out where she was.

"Aye, she's in Berlin," her mum said. "And she's not coming back to Tyneside, hen. She dropped out of the course. You're the one who made that video, aren't you? Did you know it's being shown on MTV?" Colin didn't. But the Union bar had MTV and it was true, they were showing the Pond Life video occasionally, in a late-night alternative slot. Without Jessica to share the news with, it meant little to Colin.

Word about the video soon got around. Lots of people were suddenly interested in Colin, plenty of them girls. Colin tried to enjoy his success. He went out with three or four women, but there was no spark. He didn't feel any of the closeness he'd felt to Jessica, or, for that matter, Newt. Another group asked him to do a video for them but he refused, preferring to work on a short film. Maybe that would impress Jessica, if he ever saw her again.

But Jessica wasn't interested any more. A

card on his birthday, that was the most contact he had all year. As the summer vacation approached, Colin dreading going home. What if Jessica was there? Worse, what if she wasn't? He did brilliantly in his mid-semester exams, but couldn't find a vacation job working on a documentary series, as he'd hoped. All the directors he liked seemed to be away all summer.

It was the last week of term. Colin was about to take up an offer to be a trainee assistant making TV ads. Any commercial experience was better than none, especially after he'd failed to work the previous summer. Then he was called to the phone on his corridor.

"Make it quick, Col. They're calling from America."

The voice on the other end of the line was Newt's.

"How are you?" he asked, adding honestly, "I've missed you, Newt."

"I've missed you, too," she said, "but I'm fine. And it's not Newt any more. It's Sandy. I'm about to go on tour."

"With Pond Life?"

"No. We split up. I'm with a new band.

We've got a record deal. Listen. There's a budget for a tour video and the record company liked the one you did for Pond Life. Would you be interested?"

"Would I?" Colin asked, incredulously.

"Great. I said you'd probably work cheap provided we flew you over and paid your living expenses. But maybe you've got a job already."

"I was about to accept one. Listen, I've just got one question."

"Don't tell me," Newt said, in a rueful voice, "it's – 'can your girlfriend come?' – only if she pays her own expenses."

"She isn't my girlfriend any more," Colin explained. "Actually, what I wanted to ask was whether you're ... with somebody." There was a long pause. Colin didn't know whether Sandy was showing her pride or preparing to let him down gently.

"Left it a bit late, haven't you?" she said, after at least a dollar's worth of silence.

"Does that mean 'yes'?"

"No. It means why don't you drag your butt over here and find out for yourself. Or is it too far to go?"

Colin thought for a moment. All that distance. The band always on tour, or recording. He had a degree to finish. The relationship had no chance, no chance at all.

"I'm on my way," he told her.

The Snow Queen

Robyn Turner

Melanie James had something of a reputation at the sixth-form college where she was studying A-level English Literature, German and French. It wasn't a particularly bad reputation, but it was a reputation. Kinder people called her distant and withdrawn; the more vicious called her snooty and aloof. And, as winter drew in, others (usually boys) called her the Snow Queen.

It was a reputation which wasn't entirely undeserved. Melanie was seventeen, a tall girl with raven-coloured hair which she always wore in a stylish bob, skin the colour of fine porcelain, and clothes which, no matter how baggy they were, couldn't disguise her slim and shapely figure. In short, she was the sort of person plainer girls hated, and any boy would have been proud to have been seen with.

However, in the twelve months since she

had arrived at college, she had hardly socialized at all. She seemed to spend all her time with her nose (pretty, perky, the kind a film star would kill for) in her books, and the few times a boy plucked up the courage to ask her out, she would smile weakly and refuse his offer. She'd even turned down Steve Devereaux, widely acknowledged to be the hunk of the college, and Steve's ego had never really recovered after that.

Melanie kept very much to herself, and lived with her divorced mother in one of the poshest areas of town. "She obviously thinks she's too good for the likes of us," people would say, although it didn't stop most of the boys making a play for her at one time or another.

Yet Melanie seemed to freeze in the presence of all those boys who were very sexy indeed, even though they so obviously thought that they were God's gift to the entire female species. The girls were secretly delighted that Melanie didn't show much interest in boys – it meant less competition after all – but she still had few girlfriends. Melanie wouldn't let anyone get close to her, and people often wondered why.

One of her few friends, however, was Carolanne, who made up for her plain-jane looks with a bright and vivacious personality which all the boys seemed to like. (The fact that her father was the entertainments manager of the town hall, and the source of free tickets to top-name rock gigs also had something to do with it.)

Carolanne had originally met Melanie when she wanted some help with her French homework, and Melanie had grudgingly agreed. From then on Carolanne had become intrigued by Melanie. For someone who was supposedly the Snow Queen she empathized so strongly with some of the most passionate characters in their French texts.

More than once Carolanne had spotted a small tear in the corner of Melanie's eye when she was reading a romantic passage in some book or other. It was then that Carolanne had the strangest feeling that Melanie was putting up some sort of front to the world, and that if only people could break through that frosty exterior they would find a warm and tender person beneath. But why had she adopted this frosty demeanour? And what would it take to melt it?

If she had been a more inquisitive girl, Carolanne would have asked Melanie outright, but Carolanne believed that people should be allowed their privacy. If Melanie wanted to behave the way she did, as long as it didn't affect her friendship with Carolanne, then that was her own business.

As time went on and Melanie relaxed more in Carolanne's presence, so the two girls became friendlier, although they stopped at sharing certain intimacies. Melanie appreciated Carolanne's warm and ready humour and Carolanne, for her part, enjoyed being seen in the company of someone as attractive to the boys as Melanie. She joked that the boys would try it on with Melanie and, when that failed, she'd always be able to snatch them up for herself.

"They may be your leftovers, Mel," she laughed when they were sharing a pre-Christmas drink in one of the trendy café-bars they frequented. "But they're still boys!"

"You can have them," Melanie snorted contemptuously. "They're only interested in one thing."

Carolanne looked strangely at Melanie

then, as if trying to discover a secret in those deep blue eyes. Melanie continued:

"All they're concerned with is what lies on the surface, never with what's underneath," she said sadly.

"I guess it's kind of hard being beautiful," Carolanne replied, only half-jokingly. You wouldn't hear her complaining with looks like that!

Melanie smiled. It was a wonderful smile, and one that she rarely allowed people to see. "Sorry, Carolanne," she said. "Sometimes, I don't realize how I must sound."

You've got that one right! Carolanne thought.

"Why don't you ever go out with boys?" Carolanne asked, and sipped at her glass of white wine and soda. "You could have anyone you want."

"I don't have time," Melanie protested. Her fingers tapped nervously on her glass. "I am doing three A-levels, you know."

Carolanne wasn't fooled for a moment. She knew how clever Melanie was – her three subjects posed no problem for her at all. She decided to change the conversation.

"How's your mum?" she asked. "Is she looking forward to Christmas?"

"Yes. It'll be a quiet one this time, just her and me..."

Carolanne yawned. "Quiet Christmases, I hate 'em! That's what we have at home every single year. Just me, Mum and Dad trying to be nice to each other and falling out by the time of the Queen's Speech!"

Melanie smiled. "You're lucky your parents are still married," she said wistfully.

"Messy divorce, huh?" Carolanne asked sympathetically. Melanie nodded.

"Mum got a good settlement from Dad – that's how we can afford to live in the area we do," she revealed. "But I really do miss Dad."

"Don't you see him?" Carolanne asked.

"Of course," Melanie replied. "But it's not the same. I just wish they were still together, that's all. It seems that everything I love is taken away from me sooner or later..."

Carolanne had never heard Melanie talk like this before, and she wasn't quite sure how she should react. For a moment she thought that Melanie might have had one too many glasses of wine. Then she remembered that she was drinking orange juice. Carolanne liked the occasional glass of white wine, but she had never seen Melanie touch alcohol.

There was a moment's silence as Melanie looked out of the window and at the snow falling in the street outside. Then she turned back to Carolanne.

"And I wish I was an only child like you," she said.

"Your sisters aren't coming to see you this year?" Carolanne asked. She vaguely recalled Melanie once telling her that she had three sisters, all of them several years older than her and working or studying at university.

When Melanie told her that no, they weren't, Carolanne joked that it was probably just as well. She'd get all the Christmas presents to herself, rather than having to share them with three other people.

Melanie froze, and even Carolanne was surprised by this reaction. "You're wrong Carolanne," Melanie said. "I've only got two sisters."

"But I thought you told me once..."

"*Two* sisters, Carolanne," Melanie said sharply, in a tone that invited no argument.

Carolanne frowned. She was convinced that Melanie had once told her that she had

three sisters. Angie, Caroline and … and …
and what was that other one called? Still, it
wasn't worth arguing about, and Carolanne
decided not to pursue the subject.

"A panto? I am not going to a panto!" Melanie
protested, a few days after Christmas when
Carolanne called round to Melanie's house.

Carolanne looked distressed. "C'mon, it'll
be fun. And since Dad's the entertainments
manager we won't have to pay for the
tickets," she said, and handed Melanie the
colour advertisement she'd cut out of the
local newspaper. This year's panto was
Beauty and the Beast.

"I've work to do for next term," Melanie
insisted. "What with A-levels coming up
and everything."

"Don't give me that one!" Carolanne said.
"I know you much too well. You probably
did all your holiday homework in the first
week, unlike me who'll do it on the last
night of the holidays."

Melanie chuckled: Carolanne was right,
as usual. She looked at the garishly-
coloured advertisement. It seemed to be the
usual panto fare, mixing some well-known
faces with second-rate light entertainment

performers. One face particularly took her eye – a handsome, square-jawed man with the sort of looks she'd thought existed only in the pages of upmarket fashion magazines. He looked vaguely familiar.

"Aha! That's Tim Duncan!" Carolanne said, and told Melanie that he was the star of a popular Australian TV soap opera.

Melanie, who never watched such programmes, was none the wiser. "So what's he doing in panto?" she asked. "It's a bit of a comedown, isn't it?"

"He's left his soap and is trying to break into the theatre and music biz big time," Carolanne explained knowledgeably. "I met him once about a year ago when he played a small gig over here. Dad got me backstage to say hello to him. And believe me, if you think he's just to-die-for gorgeous, wait till you see him in the flesh!"

"I guess he's OK if you like that sort of thing," Melanie said, and Carolanne nodded her head: "that sort of thing" she couldn't see enough of!

Melanie smiled, and handed the newspaper back to her friend. Sometimes she could read Carolanne like a book.

"And I suppose you've got backstage

passes?" she asked.

"Hey, Dad does have some uses, you know," Carolanne said, and tugged at Melanie's arm, like a little puppy begging to go for a walk. "C'mon, Mel, it'll be fun!"

Melanie finally gave in, knowing that Carolanne wouldn't shut up until she did. Carolanne clapped her hands triumphantly.

"I can hardly wait," she said and then shivered. "Just think – we're going to meet Tim Duncan!"

"Who knows?" Melanie joked. "He may be bowled over by you."

"He wasn't the last time we met," Carolanne reflected philosophically.

"People change – some people anyway," Melanie said a little sadly, and then brightened up. "Maybe he'll see you in a new light and you'll end up becoming Mrs Duncan!"

"That would be heavenly," Carolanne gushed, and sneaked a sly look at her friend. There was no way that Carolanne would ever stand a chance with the dreamy Tim. He was way, way out of her league. But Melanie and Tim? Now, that was another matter. Carolanne was determined that she was going to find a boy who could crack the Ice Maiden's heart if it was the last thing she did!

Melanie stood up and left the room to collect some books for Carolanne, asking her to put on the coffee in the kitchen. Melanie's mother was there, organizing that evening's meal, and Carolanne smiled at her and started to make small talk.

"Did you have a good Christmas, Mrs James?" she asked pleasantly.

"Nice but quiet," the older woman replied, as she put a small casserole into the oven. "It was the first time my other three weren't here with me."

"Your other three?" Carolanne asked.

"Yes," Mrs James replied. "My other three daughters. They're all down in London now, sharing that untidy flat of theirs. It was their first Christmas away from home."

"But I thought Melanie only had two sisters," Carolanne said, remembering what Melanie had told her.

"No, she definitely has three!" Mrs James responded.

"Are you sure?"

Melanie's mother grinned. "Angela, Caroline and Isabel," she said. "I think I should know how many daughters I have, don't you?"

"I must have been mistaken then," Carol-anne said.

Why had Melanie told her she only had two sisters? What was she trying to hide? Carolanne chose to keep her counsel: Melanie would tell her in her own good time.

"Wasn't the show great?" Carolanne asked the following night as the final curtain went down on the cast of *Beauty and the Beast*, and she and Melanie followed the other members of the audience towards the exit.

"Fine – if you like that sort of thing," Melanie quipped once more.

In fact, she had enjoyed the panto much more than she had expected. There had been the required amount of diabolical jokes, plenty of slapstick for the kids, and enough sexiness for the older members of the audience.

Tim Duncan's performance had been impressive too, even though the beast mask he wore couldn't disguise his classic good looks – as the adoring teen screams from the audience proved whenever he stepped out on to the stage.

When they were out of the theatre, Carolanne led Melanie towards the back of the building where the stage door was located. A light snow was falling, but the weather wasn't particularly cold for the time of the year. A giggling group of autograph hunters were already crowding around the door, waiting for a glimpse of their Australian hero.

They looked on in wide-eyed admiration – and green-eyed envy – as Melanie and Carolanne showed their backstage passes to the security guard and were waved on through the door.

Many of them guessed that Melanie must be Tim's girlfriend. After all, only someone as gorgeous and as sophisticated as Melanie could be good enough for their Tim. On the other hand, Carolanne had managed to get herself a backstage pass too, so maybe there was hope for them as well!

Backstage was all hustle and bustle as people rushed from dressing room to dressing room and stage hands packed away their gear for another night. As people prepared to leave they would give their colleagues – male or female, it didn't matter – a parting kiss. Melanie turned to Carolanne, and tried to look disapproving.

"Does everybody snog everybody else around here?" she asked, pretending to sound shocked. "Are they oversexed or what?"

"That's what showbiz people do!" Carolanne whispered, unaware that she was being made fun of. "It doesn't mean anything at all."

She led the way through the maze of passageways behind the stage to Tim's dressing room. As they passed, people looked at them curiously, wondering who they might be.

"We can't just barge in unannounced like this!" Melanie hissed as Carolanne raised her hand to knock on Tim's dressing-room door.

"Why ever not?" Carolanne said, and rapped loudly three times. "Dad told him to expect us!"

From the other side of the door Tim Duncan asked them to enter. His Australian tones sounded warm and friendly, conjuring up visions of romantic nights by the beach and warm and lazy days by the pool. It was a total contrast to the winter weather outside. Carolanne grinned at Melanie and then opened the door.

Tim Duncan stood up to greet them. He had changed from his beast costume into his normal clothes – a stylish designer T-shirt, a pendant around his neck, and baggy combats tucked into a pair of DMs which he'd probably paid a fortune to have scuffed up just so. His jet-black hair, which he wore just over his collar, had been slicked back, and he looked every inch the rich-boy actor from Down Under trying to prove his street cred in the UK.

"Hi," he said politely. "You're Carolanne, aren't you? We met a while back, I think, when your dad was arranging a gig here. He told me to expect you tonight."

He walked – swaggered would probably have been a better word – over to Carolanne, and kissed her on the cheek showbiz-style. Carolanne felt herself go weak at the knees: if only the girls at school could see her now, they'd go wild with envy!

"H-hi, Tim," Carolanne replied, trying – and failing – to sound cool and collected in the presence of such a hunky star.

Tim turned to Melanie and fixed her with his big blue eyes. He smiled a welcome, displaying a row of perfect teeth that gleamed as brightly as the warm Australian sun.

"And this is?" he asked, and, before Melanie could utter a word, Carolanne said:

"This is Melanie James, one of my best friends."

"Great to meet you, Melanie," Tim said and moved forward to kiss her hello.

Melanie, however, stepped back instinctively, so that Tim's lips merely brushed her cheek. Tim noticed her reluctance, and a twinkle appeared in his eyes. There was nothing Tim Duncan liked better than a challenge, especially when the challenge was as beautiful as Melanie James!

"And did you like the show, Melanie?" Tim asked, giving her the look which he knew could melt any woman's heart and turn even the most cynical punter into his adoring fan.

"It was very professionally put together, Mr Duncan," she began.

"Tim, please."

"It was very professional, Tim," Melanie continued in a toneless voice that held no warmth in it at all. "Even though it's not quite my sort of thing. I prefer stuff like Shakespeare and Molière and—"

"Yeah, I've heard of those guys," Tim interrupted before she could go any further.

Unnoticed by either Tim or Melanie, Carolanne raised her eyes heavenwards in dismay. What game was Melanie playing here? she asked herself. Here she was with the most fantastic-looking guy from daytime telly coming on to her and she was freezing him out by talking about cruddy old dead playwrights! What was with that frosty tone of voice?

Suddenly there was a knock at the door, and a boy about Melanie and Carolanne's age walked in. He was tall and slim, certainly not even half as muscular as Tim, and his mousy-brown hair fell in front of his eyes in a long fringe.

There was a babyish and vulnerable quality about his face; he reminded Carolanne of the lead singer of one of the bands popular at the moment. Carolanne wasn't a big fan of those groups; they seemed to sing about nothing but urban decay and boring social issues, when all she really wanted to hear about was love.

"We're ready when you are, Tim," the newcomer said, and Tim nodded.

"I'll be right out, Marc," he said and

introduced the newcomer as Marc Barker, one of the soundcheck men on the show.

Marc said hello to the two girls and held out his hand for them to shake. He seemed nervous of meeting strangers, Melanie noticed, and when he shook her hand he turned his eyes away from her. As he did so his hair flopped engagingly over his eyes. Marc smiled and then left the dressing room.

"We're all going off to Slippery Slopes for a late-night drink," Tim said, referring to a trendy café-club that was frequented by theatricals. "Do you two girls want to come?"

"Do we ever!" Carolanne said, and when she caught sight of Melanie looking doubt-fully at her watch, added sternly: "And you are coming as well, Melanie! You can't use school tomorrow as an excuse. We're still in the Christmas holidays."

"OK," Melanie said. "But I won't be drinking anything alcoholic."

"It's a private club, you'll be OK," Tim said and took each girl by the arm.

"It's not that, Tim," she said. "But I never drink. It's one of the little rules I've made for myself."

Tim and Carolanne exchanged despairing glances. What other rules did Melanie have, they wanted to know.

"He's crazy about you!" Carolanne said, and Melanie looked around to see who Carolanne was talking about. Slippery Slopes was packed full of members of the cast and crew of the panto, plus several fans who seemed to have slipped past security and were making eyes at their hero from the far corner of the room.

"Who? Tim?" Melanie asked and yawned.

The Ozzie star had been chatting her up for most of the evening now, and, if the truth were known, he was boring her to tears. His sole subject of conversation seemed to be himself, or his career, and not once had he asked her about herself.

He'd made a point of putting his arm around her, however, especially when some of his best buddies had passed by and looked on enviously. At that moment he'd left their table and was collecting some drinks from the bar.

"Of course, Tim is," Carolanne said. "But he's not the one I'm talking about."

She nodded over to Marc who was sitting

with some friends at another table. When he saw them looking at him he turned away shyly.

"Marc is?" asked Melanie.

"Is that his name?" Carolanne said, and then giggled. "I'd forgotten. I mean, when you're in the same room as Tim Duncan nothing else seems to matter."

"Carolanne, don't be so superficial," Melanie reproved her and looked back at Marc. "He's sort of sweet, isn't he?"

Carolanne's reply clearly proved that she thought her friend had lost her mind.

"*Him?* Are you kidding?" She turned and considered Marc for a moment before saying: "Well, I suppose he's not *that* bad-looking... But no matter how cute he is he simply can't compare to someone like Tim."

"Looks aren't everything," Melanie said. "Personality counts for much more."

"And what a personality Tim has!" Carolanne enthused. "So manly, so forceful and confident. That guy there – what's his name again? – looks about as interesting as a wet weekend in Wigan!"

"Maybe he's just shy," Melanie said, and continued looking at Marc. He looked back at her, and then quickly turned away again. Melanie smiled to herself.

"You don't even know him, and it looks as though you never will now," Carolanne said. "He's leaving."

Marc had stood up and was helping his neighbour – a pretty and petite red-headed dancer in the show – on with her coat. Their exit towards the door made them pass by Melanie and Carolanne's table, and Marc paused, hesitated, and then stopped to say goodbye to the two of them.

"You should have come over," Melanie told him.

Marc coloured slightly. "You seemed so taken up with Tim," he said. "I didn't want to disturb you…"

"There was nothing to disturb," Melanie reassured him. Was it her imagination or did his eyes light up beneath that Brit Pop fringe of his?

There was an awkward pause. The girl Marc was accompanying tapped her foot impatiently. She was obviously in a rush to get home. Finally, the two of them said their goodbyes and left the club. Melanie and Carolanne watched them go.

"He's sweet," Melanie said. "And so polite.

He doesn't push himself on people – unlike some other guys I could mention."

Carolanne looked curiously at her friend. There was a warmth in Melanie's voice she'd never heard before. And whereas Melanie normally tried to avoid boys' attention she had seemed to be positively encouraging Marc!

"Just don't let his girlfriend hear you say that," Carolanne chuckled, referring to the red-headed girl on Marc's arm.

Melanie nodded. "Of course, he has a girlfriend, hasn't he?"

And suddenly a wave of melancholy swept over Melanie James and she had an almost irresistible desire to burst into tears. Yet she didn't cry, for to cry was a sign of weakness, and Melanie had vowed that she would never cry again.

And the tears she wanted to cry were not over Marc.

About half an hour later Melanie decided that she had had enough of the party and wanted to go home. Both Carolanne and (especially) Tim urged her to stay, but when they realized that there would be no persuading her, Tim offered to order her a cab.

("Hey, Mel, there's no prob – I can easily afford to give you the fare," he said, and waved a wad of notes in her direction.)

Melanie declined. She needed some time to think for herself, she told them, and she enjoyed walking through the streets alone. It was only snowing lightly outside and since she lived just a few blocks away she knew that she'd be perfectly safe.

As she left the club, she became aware of a figure standing in the shadows. For a moment Melanie panicked, thinking that she was in danger, but then the figure stepped out from the shadows and into the streetlight where she could see him better. Melanie breathed a sigh of relief.

"I hope I didn't frighten you," Marc said, and Melanie relaxed. There were snowflakes in Marc's brown hair and in the cold his cheeks were red. Or at least she thought it was the cold that had made him blush.

"Marc, what are you doing here?" she asked.

Once again Marc lowered his face so as not to look into Melanie's eyes. "I ... I just thought I'd come back and rejoin the party."

"But I thought you'd gone back home with your girlfriend."

Marc looked up. "Cressida's just a friend, she's not my girlfriend," he said urgently.

Melanie wondered why her heart leapt in her breast at that piece of news. "I'm sorry. I got the idea when I saw you holding hands as you went out..."

Marc laughed. It was an attractive laugh, like the sound of sleigh bells on Christmas morning.

"Cressida's a good mate, that's all," he told her. "She wants to be an actress eventually. Calls everyone 'darling', is totally tactile with everybody. That's just the way she behaves: real showbiz!"

Marc turned away shyly from her again. *What's got into him?* Melanie wondered. *He's so unlike Tim and all those other boys...* She shivered.

"It's cold standing here," she said, and looked at Marc until he was forced to return her gaze.

"What are you doing now?" Marc finally plucked up the courage to ask.

"I'm going home," she told him. "The club back there was getting a bit too noisy for me."

"For me too," Marc said. "I hate loud clubs and music."

(*So why were you coming back?* Melanie wondered, but remained silent.)

Another awkward silence followed, with each of them shuffling their feet, unwilling to leave the other.

"Why don't you walk me home?" Melanie suggested eventually. "I only live a few blocks away from here."

Marc smiled from ear to ear. "Walk you home ... you ... well, yeah, sure," he managed to stammer out.

"Don't worry, I won't bite," Melanie said, and offered him her arm. "Take me by the arm – like show people do."

"Yeah, sure," Marc said and took her arm and escorted her down the street.

Melanie smiled, as they walked arm in arm through the snow. Marc tried not to press too close to her body – fearing that might give her the wrong impression – and he made sure that she avoided all the icy patches on the pavement where she might slip and hurt herself.

Marc started talking nineteen-to-the-dozen, asking her about herself, what were her favourite bands, did she have any brothers and sisters?

"Two, both of whom live down in London,"

she replied.

"That's great," Marc said. "Families are so important, aren't they? I don't know what I'd do without mine."

Marc seemed nervous, as many people do when they're with a very beautiful person. He started to talk about inconsequential subjects, about the weather, about TV, about a thousand-and-one things, about anything other than the one thing he wanted to speak about.

"Cressida's a nice name," Melanie remarked, as they turned the corner and started to walk up the hill which led to her house. They'd been talking about how Cressida used to flirt with Tim when the panto had first come to town. "It comes from Shakespeare, doesn't it?"

"That's right," Marc said. *"Troilus and Cressida."* He pulled a face. "Not exactly my favourite play."

Melanie turned and smiled at Marc. "I wouldn't have thought you'd like Shakespeare," she said.

"I love him," Marc said with enthusiasm. "I might only be a sound technician now, but what I really want to be is an actor. Cressida often helps me out with my lines after the show. I've an audition down in London in a few weeks' time for drama school. I don't hold out much hope of getting in though."

"You should have more confidence in yourself," Melanie told him. *If you had, you'd've come over to my table; then Tim Duncan wouldn't have bored me to death all evening!* she thought. "One of my sisters down in London is studying to be an actress."

"Really? Where's she studying?" Marc asked. "Maybe she could give me a few tips on how to handle an audition?"

"She's studying at—" Melanie began and then corrected herself. "No, how stupid of me. She gave up the course last year. Neither of my two sisters studies drama..."

Melanie felt an unbearable sadness well up in her heart. And now she really did want to cry: she suddenly felt so wretched lying to Marc. "We're home now."

She looked up at the posh house on the hill, its houselights all turned up bright. It looked so cold and uninviting, while the real warmth was out here in the snow with this insecure and strangely vulnerable boy.

"Well, I guess I'll be going then..." Marc said.

"Thanks for walking me home, Marc..."

"It was my pleasure. Well, it was nice talking to you, Melanie ... and..."

"Yes?"

"Oh, nothing..." He turned to go.

"Aren't you going to give me a goodnight kiss?" Melanie asked, and then added, "Showbiz-style of course."

"Of course," Marc said, and kissed Melanie once, twice, three times on the cheeks.

And then there was a pause as he stared into her eyes. His face was only inches away from hers as they exchanged a look, a look the meaning of which each of them recognized.

"Goodnight, Melanie," Marc said. He turned to go, then paused, and looked shyly at Melanie again. "'Goodnight, goodnight! Parting is such sweet sorrow'," he quoted mischievously.

"'That I shall say goodnight till it be morrow'," Melanie finished, recognizing the quotation. "*Romeo and Juliet!* My favourite play!"

"Mine as well," Marc grinned. "Now I really do have to go."

"Good night, Marc," Melanie said sadly, and watched Marc's departing figure trudging through the snow.

And it was then that Melanie James knew that she had fallen hopelessly in love.

And she was very, very scared. She shook her head, and hugged herself for warmth. It couldn't be happening, not again, she told herself over and over again. She had promised herself, told herself she would never reach out for another boy ever again, and certainly not for someone like Marc. For Melanie knew that when you give your love to another, then sure as anything you got yourself hurt.

And Melanie would never let herself be hurt ever again.

Holding back the sobs, she turned, and went into the house and locked the door behind her.

"You want to see the panto again!" Carolanne asked in disbelief, when Melanie phoned her up the following morning. "Aha! I know what you're planning, Mel! It's not *Beauty and the Beast* you want to see, it's Tim Duncan! You've got the hots for him, haven't you?"

"The hots for him?" Melanie repeated and Carolanne apologized. Melanie James was certainly not the sort of girl who would get "the hots" for anyone!

Melanie continued, "As far as I'm concerned there are far nicer people in the world than Tim Duncan."

On the other end of the line the penny dropped for Carolanne. "That sound technician guy? Oh, Mel, how could you?"

"His name's Marc and he's sweet and he's cultured and he's kind and – "

– "and compared to Tim Duncan he's nothing – "

– "and he's so different to everyone else," Melanie continued. "I know he likes me, but he doesn't try to push himself upon me. He's not full of himself like Tim and all those other boys, and he's actually interested in me for a change – and not just his masculine ego. Do you realize how tiresome it is having boys like Tim come on to me all the time?"

"I should be so lucky," Carolanne joked.

"And besides I like him as a friend, that's all," Melanie claimed. "If you think I'm going to do anything as stupid as fall in love with him then you're totally wrong!"

"Did I even mention love?" Carolanne asked. She didn't believe Melanie for one second. She agreed to come to the panto with her again, though.

"Darling, you were absolutely marvellous!" Cressida cooed, and planted a huge kiss on Marc's lips. "The sound tonight was so crisp, so perfect, so deep – just like you, in fact."

Marc smiled awkwardly and looked over to the backstage area where Melanie and Carolanne were approaching them. He waved nervously at them, and Cressida got the hint and walked away. Marc went up to the two girls and kissed them on the cheeks (showbiz-style, of course).

"Melanie, you've come back!" he said, and also nodded a welcome to Carolanne. He led them to a place away from the backstage noise and activity where they could talk better. "It's so nice to see you again."

"And you too..."

Carolanne sighed. She was feeling distinctly out of place here already. She made her apologies and left, making a beeline for Tim's dressing room. After all, she told herself, nothing ventured, nothing gained!

"I just wondered what you were doing after the show tonight?" Melanie asked, and Marc looked strangely at her.

"Are you making fun of me?" he asked warily.

"Of course not," Melanie said. "Why should I do that?"

"Oh, no reason," he said unsurely. "It's just that it's not that often that girls ask me out on a date."

"I didn't say it was a date," Melanie corrected him. "I just wondered what your plans were for the next couple of hours, that's all."

Marc beamed. "I was supposed to be studying my audition piece for drama school," he said, and then sighed. "But what's the point? Like I said, I probably won't get it."

"You've no reason to say that," Melanie said.

"I never seem to get what I want in this life," Marc said, and affected a little-boy expression. "Besides you've never seen me act!"

"Don't put yourself down," Melanie told him. "I bet you're really good – you just haven't realized it yet. Like you haven't realized some other things either."

"Such as?"

"Never mind."

That you're gorgeous and modest and self-effacing and that not all girls like swaggering and muscle-bound hunks like Tim Duncan and co.! is what Melanie thought.

They waited around for Carolanne and, when she finally appeared, she informed them that all the gang were going to Slippery Slopes again.

Melanie and Marc exchanged looks – they didn't like that idea at all. Carolanne regarded them curiously but finally accepted their excuse that they didn't have enough money to afford the club's inflated prices and anyway they didn't want to give Tim the opportunity to show off and lend them some money.

Instead they found a pleasant and inexpensive café-bar just around the corner from the theatre. As they shuffled into their corner seat, several boys looked enviously at Marc and his companion. Melanie also noticed, with pleasure, that some girls were looking appreciatively at Marc. She pointed this out to him, but he refused to believe her, while at the same time being secretly delighted.

Melanie had suggested that Marc bring his audition piece with him, and, as they shared a couple of Diet Cokes and a bottle of mineral water, he would quote passages from *Romeo and Juliet* to her across the table. Marc had a wonderful phrasing and, as he spoke Shakespeare's words of love, they seemed to be directed just at her.

They spent the next two hours talking and, once his defences were lowered, Melanie found Marc very easy to chat to. For some reason she seemed to be able to put him at ease, and he made her laugh with his tales of backstage life.

Occasionally, when he passed her the bottle of Evian, for instance, or when he brought her a glass of orange juice from the bar, their hands would brush lightly against each other. It was then that a frisson of pleasure ran through Melanie's body. Their legs would sometimes touch under the table as well, and they would hurriedly move them away, while feeling that same electric surge of joy.

By the time closing time came around and

Marc took Melanie's arm – showbiz-style of course – and led her out into the chilly, snow-covered street, they both knew exactly what was about to happen. It seemed inevitable as night following day, as the tide rushing to shore. Neither of them had mentioned it in the café, but then there are certain things in this world that are beyond mere words.

As the snow fell all around them, they kissed, a long lingering kiss. Melanie drew Marc to her, running her fingers through his hair, and stroking back the fringe from his beautiful blue eyes. Those eyes smiled down at her, soft and adoring, and so unlike the lascivious looks other boys had given her.

Marc pulled away from her for a second, and smiled. "Beauty and the Beast," he chuckled. Melanie frowned: what did he mean?

"I never thought that someone as beautiful as you would even give the likes of me a second look," he said. "I'm not as good-looking as Tim Duncan or any of the other boys you probably go out with."

"I don't go out with anyone else, Marc," Melanie said and her eyes misted over with unshed tears. "And beauty is only skin-deep. It's what's inside that really matters."

"You're making all my dreams come true, do you know that, Melanie?" Marc breathed and kissed her again. "You're the best thing that ever happened to me."

This time he held her even closer, as though he would never let her go. The light from the streetlamp shone in his hair, and made the snow seem like a halo around his head. He was an angel, Melanie realized, her guardian angel come to take her away from her life of loneliness and despair, an angel come to melt her cold and hurting heart.

Suddenly all her past life seemed to have been but a dream, nothing more than an unpleasant nightmare from which she had just awoken. This was the only reality: just her and Marc, and the snow falling all around them, cutting them off from the rest of the shabby little world, blessing them with its downy touch and promising them true and eternal love. Melanie felt tears welling up in her eyes, but they were tears not of hurt but of joy.

Finally the angel found the confidence and the courage to speak the words he'd been longing to utter ever since he'd first caught sight of Melanie in Tim's dressing room.

"Melanie, I..."

Melanie gazed up into Marc's eyes. "Yes, Marc?" she asked.

"I... I..."

Melanie smiled fondly. They had no need of words now, not these two, and Melanie knew exactly what Marc was trying to tell her. Yet she closed her eyes, as though adding her strength to his, willing him to speak the words she had been longing to hear for so long.

"I love you," he said at last, and then added ironically: "There – I've finally said it."

"And I..." Melanie began, and then halted. Why were those three words so difficult for her? Marc was different, he wasn't like all the others. She trusted him, she had to trust him. She had to sacrifice her fears, forget the past and all that hurt, for his sake.

"And I love you too." Melanie said.

Suddenly she froze and pulled away.

"Melanie, what's wrong?" Marc asked, and his voice was full of concern.

"You do love me, don't you?" Melanie asked, almost warily. Her voice was trembling now.

"Of course I do," Marc said. "I've just said that."

"And Cressida?"

Marc smiled kindly. "I told you, Cressida is just a mate who helps me out with my acting lessons sometimes," he reassured her. "I'm not even her type – remember how I told you how she used to flirt with Tim? There's only you, Melanie. There will only ever be you."

"I just wanted to be certain..." she said, but she knew from the look in Marc's eyes that he was telling the truth. Eyes such as his couldn't deceive, they were incapable of lying. Weren't they?

Marc chucked her under the chin. "It's not like you to be so unsure of yourself," he said. "How could anyone not fall hopelessly in love with someone as beautiful as you?"

Melanie turned her head away so that Marc couldn't see the sadness in her eyes.

"I just ... I just don't want to be hurt, that's all," she said finally. Marc turned her face so that she was looking at him.

"I'll never hurt you, Melanie," he promised.

I'll never hurt you, Mel, she heard some-one else say in her mind. But that was a long time ago now. And yet the pain was still there, gnawing at her heart.

No, the past is the past! Melanie told herself sternly. *Learn to trust! Learn to love again!*

"You'll never leave me?" she asked Marc.

"Never as long as I live," he said, and then pulled Melanie even closer to him.

And while Melanie melted into his arms, and gave in to all those passions that she had kept checked for so long, there was still a nagging doubt in the back of her mind. For Melanie was just as insecure as the boy she now held lovingly in her arms.

Please let it be all right, she said to herself over and over again. *Please don't let it be like the last time... Don't let me be hurt again...*

As the weeks passed, and the panto drew nearer to its close, so Melanie and Marc's love for each other grew and grew. They spent almost every waking hour of the day together, and when they were apart at night they shared their dreams of each other.

Even the spurned Tim had to admit that they looked good together, as Melanie waited for Marc every night by the stage door. Cressida, however, was particularly cold towards Melanie, and occasionally Melanie wondered just what there was between her and Marc. Had he and Cressida once had something together? Was that why Cressida was now being so unfriendly towards her? *No*, Melanie kept telling herself, *Marc told me that she's just a mate, and he wouldn't lie to me, would he? He wouldn't be like the others...*

Marc had noticed Melanie's disquiet and had told her that Cressida was irritated with her taking up all his time – it meant that she couldn't practise her own audition pieces with Marc as often as she used to.

Still that nagging doubt kept coming back to Melanie. Sometimes she would wonder if that was the only reason. But one look into Marc's eyes told her all she needed to know.

"You've done so much for me," Marc told her one night, as he held her hand in the small corner café that only they knew about. A copy of *Romeo and Juliet* lay on the table – Marc had finally decided on his audition piece for drama school: Romeo's very first meeting with Juliet. "Going out with you has built up my confidence so much."

"Nonsense," Melanie said. Marc silenced her.

"Before I met you I always compared myself with people like Tim," he confessed. "Tim seemed to have no trouble meeting girls, whereas I used to come over all tongue-tied and shy. Tim used to get all the girls."

"Tim did not get *this* girl," Melanie reminded him, and squeezed his hand even more tightly. She kissed him lightly on the lips. Just the touch and the taste of him sent shivers down her spine.

"I'm going down to London for my audition at drama school, just as soon as the panto ends," he reminded her. "You will wait for me, won't you?"

Melanie laughed. "You'll be gone two days," she said. "I think that even I can hold out that long."

"You could always come down with me," he said and winked at her. "We could make it our very first holiday together."

Melanie shuddered involuntarily. "No, Marc, don't ask me to do that," she said.

"What's wrong?" he asked.

"Nothing at all," she lied. "I don't like London, that's all."

"I thought that was where your two sisters lived?" Marc said, confused.

"Besides, school's started again, and I can't afford to miss out on any lessons," Melanie continued, choosing to ignore Marc's last question.

Marc stroked her hand. "If there's anything wrong you can tell me, you know," he said. "You never talk much about your past. Is there something you're wanting to hide?"

Melanie shook her head. "There's nothing wrong, Marc," she said, and then took her hand away from his and raised it to his soft full lips. "Just promise me that you'll never leave me, that's all."

Marc kissed her fingers. "Is that what you're worried about, Melanie?" he asked tenderly. "That if I get this place in drama school then I'll move down to London and away from you?"

Melanie shrugged noncommittally, as Marc continued.

"If you feel like that, then I won't go for the audition," he said. "The panto's finishing the day after tomorrow, but I'll be able to find more work in town. All I want is to make you happy, Melanie. That's the only reason I have for living…"

"What can I do, Carolanne?" Melanie asked her friend the following morning. "If he goes to London how do I know that he'll ever come back?"

"Of course he'll come back," said Carolanne, who didn't really see what all the fuss was about. "And even if he does find digs in London he'll be able to see you at the weekends. London's only about an hour's train journey from here – it's not like it's the end of the world. He'd be a fool not to come back."

"He didn't the last time…" Melanie said.

"What do you mean?" Carolanne asked.

"Nothing," Melanie replied quickly. "This audition means so much to him, but he says he'll cancel it for me."

"He must love you a lot," Carolanne commented.

"And I love him too," Melanie said. "And I can't bear to lose him."

Carolanne put her arm around her friend's shoulder. "You're a strange one, Melanie," she said softly. "Only a few weeks ago the boys were calling you..." Her voice tailed off, but Melanie smiled.

"I know, they called me the Ice Maiden or the Snow Queen, didn't they?" she said, and a tear trickled down the side of her face. "Frosty Melanie James who'd never give even the best-looking boys the time of day let alone a date."

"You've turned down hunks who wouldn't even acknowledge my existence," Carolanne said.

"All they wanted was to show me off to their friends," Melanie said. "None of them needed me. Not like Marc does... He was so unsure of himself when we first met. But now he's gained so much confidence, and he's proved to himself that he's a good actor.

"And he's given me his love, love for me as a person and not as a thing to show off to his mates." Melanie's eyes seemed to wander off into the distance. "But there was something else too. I turned all those other boys down, because I was scared ... scared that they would leave me, like Marc might if he goes to drama school ... like last time..."

"Last time?"

The tears were flowing freely now. It was as if all the ice and hardness which had dwelt hidden inside Melanie until she had met Marc was now melting. She didn't say anything for long minutes, and, when she did, her voice was cracked and strained.

"There was a boy once, a long time ago," Melanie told Carolanne. "Handsome, strong, confident, a few years older than me: quite a hunk, in fact." She chuckled bitterly. "A lot like Tim Duncan if you must know..."

"And you loved him?"

Melanie nodded. "I loved Chris with all my heart, Carolanne, and he said he loved me too, that he'd never hurt me. Told me I was the most precious, most special thing in his life... And I believed him. And then ... and then..."

"He left you for someone else?" Carolanne guessed. *Men are such pigs*, she thought.

"He met someone else in London," Melanie said. "And ever since then I've been scared that another man will do the same thing. I decided I never wanted to be hurt like that again. So when Mum and I moved here, I vowed never to let anyone get that close to me ever again. I promised myself that never again would I love another boy." She smiled bitterly. "I became the Snow Queen, if you like. And I decided I never wanted to see again that girl who stole Chris from me. I even refused to acknowledge her existence."

"Your third sister," Carolanne suddenly realized. "She stole your boyfriend from you?"

Melanie nodded. "I loved my sister Isabel," she admitted. "But she took my Chris from me. She says it was just for one night, and that they'd both had a lot to drink—"

"And that's why you never touch alcohol," Carolanne realized.

"Isa hurt me, so as far as I'm concerned she doesn't exist," Melanie said.

"But Marc's not like this Chris," Carolanne said. "He loves you. He'd never double-cross you like that."

"How can I be sure?" Melanie asked. "How can I be so certain that it's not going to happen all over again?"

"Talk to Marc," Carolanne urged, "tell him what you've told me now. He'll understand."

"He loves his family," Melanie said, remembering their conversation on the first night he had walked her home. "How will he feel about me when he discovers that I can't even bring myself to acknowledge my own sister's existence?"

"If he loves you enough then he'll forgive you," Carolanne said. "That's what love is — knowing another person's faults and forgiving them all the same."

Melanie turned up unannounced backstage as the curtain went down on the panto later that night. She'd become such a frequent visitor that the doorman knew her by sight and waved her through.

Backstage there was a great sense of excitement. It had been a packed house, and Tim had turned in a marvellous performance, with all the little girls in the audience ooh-ing and aah-ing over his classic good looks.

Melanie smiled secretly to herself. If only they knew that beauty is just skin-deep, and that someone as sweet and as kind as Marc was worth more than a thousand Tims.

Tim passed by her on the way to his dressing room, and gave her a friendly peck on the cheek. Melanie had started to warm to the handsome Ozzie star. Since he'd realized that he didn't stand a chance with her, he had eased up in her presence, and proved that, beneath all the swagger and bravado, he was basically an OK guy.

(Tim had also stopped flirting with other members of the cast, Melanie had noticed, which she thought was pretty strange.)

She wasn't able to find Marc in the sound technician's box, and so she asked Tim where he was. He nodded towards the stage area, and then went off to his dressing room.

Melanie took a deep breath and walked towards the heavy velvet curtains. This wasn't going to be the easiest thing in her life, but she knew that Marc had to know the truth. Marc loved her and she was sure that he would understand. Trust was the most important thing in a relationship, and without trust and mutual respect there was nothing.

Chris hadn't respected her and that was why he had had his affair with her sister, Isabel. Strangely, Melanie no longer felt anything for Chris. Marc was the centre of her world now, and the past seemed a thousand centuries ago.

And she had to prove that she trusted

Marc too. She would tell him that he had to go down to London to take his audition for drama school. She knew Marc; she knew that he wouldn't leave her as Chris had done. With the love and the trust they shared, she now realized that distances meant nothing. Love such as theirs could move mountains – so what did a hundred miles or so matter?

She drew back the curtain and walked on to the empty stage. What she saw broke her heart in two.

Standing in the middle of the set of the castle from *Beauty and the Beast* were Marc and Cressida. They were holding each other in a passionate embrace, and Melanie knew instantly that this was not a typical show-people embrace.

This was the real thing, a passionate display of love and passion and romance.

And of betrayal and lies and deceit.

And of the shattering of all of Melanie's dreams, and of her new-found belief in the power of love.

Melanie turned and ran away, without Marc and Cressida even noticing her. She had been a pathetic little fool even to think that Marc had loved her. Just like every other boy she had ever known, he had used her for his own vicious purposes and then discarded her. How he and Cressida must have laughed at her, just as Isabel and Chris must have chuckled over her naïveté a year ago.

Melanie didn't even allow herself the luxury of tears. She vowed that she would never love again, that she would never be made a fool of for the rest of her life. She was through with boys, through with love.

She stormed out of the theatre, out of Marc's life for ever. And, on that cold winter's night, the Snow Queen's heart froze over once more and she knew that not even the hottest fires would ever thaw that heart again.

Melanie never returned Marc's calls, she refused to open the door when he came calling around at her house. Marc even tried to contact her through Carolanne, but, as far as Carolanne was concerned, he was scum, the creep who had broken her friend's heart, and she would have no truck with him.

So vehement was her anger that even

when Tim Duncan phoned her at home – something she could once only have dreamed of – she slammed the phone down on him. She knew that he would only try to feed her excuses for Marc's despicable behaviour. Boys were like that, always sticking up for each other when one of them had just behaved like a total scumbag.

The panto season was over now, and the cast and crew had packed up and gone their separate ways. Tim Duncan had moved down to London, and Melanie guessed that Marc would also have gone down to the capital for his audition. He'd probably win a place at drama school, she guessed.

And to think that she had helped him, giving him the confidence that he needed so much. She remembered how she had had him read his piece from *Romeo and Juliet* to her, and the passion and feeling he had put into every line. It had been just as if he was addressing her, reading out those words of love especially for her.

"'If I profane with my unworthiest hand
This holy shrine, the gentle fine is this:
My lips, two blushing pilgrims, ready stand
To smooth that rough touch with a tender kiss.'"

He had spoken those words to her the last time he had seen her, and then he had kissed her, a long and passionate kiss, which promised love and commitment and caring and—

No, he was deceiving me, conning me! Melanie corrected herself, as the doorbell rang and she got up to answer it.

She looked out through the spyhole. Carolanne was standing there. Satisfied that it wasn't Marc, she opened the door.

"Melanie, I have to talk to you," she said urgently, as she brushed the snow out of her hair. She turned around and waved to someone sitting in a flash sports car in the driveway. Tim Duncan got out and walked up the drive to Melanie and Carolanne. Someone else followed him.

Cressida! That witch who stole Marc from me! Melanie thought angrily.

"What's she doing here?" Melanie demanded.

"Can't we talk about this inside?" Tim asked, but Melanie shook her head.

"She stays outside," Melanie insisted, referring to Cressida. However, she made no movement to invite either Tim or Carolanne inside the house.

"You've got it all wrong, Mel," Carolanne said.

"Believe me," Cressida said.

"Believe you?" Melanie asked, struggling to keep her voice steady. "Believe you after you and Marc have used me? After you were carrying on behind my back?"

"Don't be ridiculous," Cressida said. "You're not thinking straight. How could Marc have used you? You were the best thing that ever happened to him. Without the confidence you gave him, he'd never have got that place at drama school."

"He's got in!" Melanie said delightedly, and then composed herself. What did it matter to her anyway? He was a louse, a cheat, not even worthy of her interest. Who cared if he got a place at drama school or not?

"He phoned me this morning," Tim said. "Just after Carolanne finally agreed to see me."

"See you?" Melanie asked and then turned angrily to Carolanne. "I thought you told me that you hung up whenever he called you?"

"He wrote to me," Carolanne told her. "He told me what was really going on."

"You don't have to tell me what was really going on! He was seeing her –" Melanie pointed at Cressida, unable even to pronounce her name – "I saw them on stage. Holding each other like they'd never let each other go."

"You saw them on stage," Carolanne said.

"So? On stage, in the street, at the club, what does it matter?" Melanie snapped.

"On stage," Tim repeated. "Remember how Cressida always helped Marc out with his acting? They were playing out a scene from *Romeo and Juliet* – that was all."

"And you seriously expect me to believe that?" Melanie demanded. Did they take her for an even bigger idiot than she already felt?

"As a matter of fact, yes," Cressida said. "Marc's a lovely and good-looking guy, but he's not my type. It's taken me a while but I've finally got the one person I want."

She reached out for Tim's hand, and looked lovingly up into his eyes.

"You and Tim?" Melanie asked in disbelief, and the two of them nodded.

Melanie remembered how she'd remarked that Tim had stopped his flirting recently. Was that because he'd started going out with Cressida? From the look the two of them exchanged it was clear that it was.

Melanie was silent for a moment, as the truth of what she had heard sank in. She had been so hurt before that she had judged the present by what had happened in the past. And in doing so she had nearly lost the one boy she loved above all others, the only boy who had really needed her.

Nearly lost? Who was to say that she hadn't lost him for good?

"I've made a total fool of myself, haven't I?" she asked.

"Yes, I'm afraid you have, Melanie," a voice said softly and without any recrimination.

Melanie looked up. Someone else had joined Carolanne, Tim and Cressida by the open door, a person she had just about given up all hope of ever seeing again.

"Marc..."

Marc was standing there, smiling affectionately at her, the handsomest man in the whole world.

"Marc, how can you ever forgive me?" Melanie asked, but Marc just stepped up to her and placed a silencing finger on her lips.

"That's what true love is all about," Marc

said. "Letting down your defences, and taking a chance and trusting someone with your whole heart. Unless you're prepared to do that then you'll never know true love. And it's also about forgiving people when they make fools of themselves, because you love them and don't ever want to see them hurt."

"I love you, Marc," Melanie said, and went to kiss him.

"And it's also about forgiving people for what they've done in the past," Marc said, and turned to another person who had just arrived, a pretty blonde several years older then Melanie. "By chance I got talking to a fellow drama student when I was auditioning. I discovered we had something in common. She'd like to see you again."

"Isa..." Melanie said, and for a moment felt nothing but hatred for the elder sister who had stolen Chris away from her. And then she realized that if she hadn't lost Chris then she would never have met Marc.

"Mel, I'm sorry," Isabel said hesitantly. "What I did was wrong, and I know it. Will you forgive me?"

For a second Melanie was inclined to say no. And then she realized that Marc was right, and she hugged her sister.

That's what love is – the love of lovers, the love of sisters, the love of friends – being able to forgive someone no matter what. Trusting them, respecting them, giving yourself up to them body and soul.

She turned to Marc and reached out for him. They held each other tightly and there were tears in both their eyes.

And love was about something else as well. It was about being beside the boy you love and adore, the boy who accepts you for what you are, and the boy with whom you know you will be spending the rest of your life.

Melanie and Marc had each taught the other an important lesson. They had drawn strength from each other, they had proved that without the other neither of them was complete. They were a team now – Melanie and Marc, Marc and Melanie – two sides of the same coin, a Romeo and Juliet whose own love story would go on for ever and ever.

And as Melanie kissed Marc – her own, dear, loving, beautiful Marc – the ice in the Snow Queen's heart finally melted.

Island Return

Sally James

"What *am* I doing back here?" Jenna thought to herself as she watched the frothy waves pound the pebbled beach. "This is the kind of thing people do in films, not real life."

She tutted. It had been her mum's idea that she get away – take a week off work for a change of scene. "Go and stay with your Gran. It's been six weeks now, love, and you're just not getting on with your life. You're not even enjoying your new job, are you?" Jenna felt an accusatory glare and detected the running-out-of-patience tone. She knew her mum was right. She should be relishing the new challenge as a legal secretary that the New Year had brought, but the truth was she felt that work, life, were getting in the way, trying to stop her thinking about Carl and their two years together, trying to distract her from feeling sad when it was all she wanted to do.

Her gran's place didn't seem far enough

away from it all. She had felt a sudden, frantic need to go far further, but to somewhere she knew. So, six weeks after that final meeting with Carl and a quick £350 later she had come back alone to Deya in Majorca, the beautiful little village on the north side of the island, with its steep narrow walkways, lively main street and the enchanting rocky cove of a beach. All the places she had discovered hand in hand with Carl last September when they had been surrounded by happy people enjoying the late summer's enclosing warmth, when the blue sky had met a crystal clear tranquil sea. The glow of the sun complemented the people in their brightly coloured clothes, their brown skin. It was all so perfect – the last place Jenna had felt totally happy with him. The little village was their special place. Reckless desperation had driven her to return, to feel it all again, to feel the memories.

As the waves crashed on to the Mediterranean shore she remembered it all for the hundredth time, how four months earlier Carl had booked a holiday with the money saved from his summer job.

"I need a break," he'd announced.

Jenna had looked surprised.

"When?... where...?"

"Majorca, and it's already booked. I've just got back from the travel agents – got a great deal. You'll have to book yours tomorrow – if you're coming with me."

Carl was studying at university and the cozy feeling she'd experienced while packing and heading for the airport had made such a pleasant change from the Sunday-evening goodbyes at the station when Carl went back to college after a weekend at home. Jenna was sick to death of watching Intercity trains float away from platform three. She'd have settled for a summer day trip somewhere, but the Mediterranean, together for two weeks; her excitement spilled over. It was lucky she could afford to pay for the holiday immediately. Carl was surprised when she revealed she had enough money tucked away.

When they were all packed he had joked at her enthusiasm.

"You're small time! It's only a package deal, nothing exotic. Some of my uni mates are going backpacking to the Far East."

Jenna rested her head on his shoulder. "I'm just happy, that's all."

The first night on the island Carl had taken her out to the pizzeria on the corner at the end of the main street. Then they had strolled back hand in hand through the evening warmth to the terracotta-roofed hotel.

"It doesn't seem like two years, does it?" Jenna had said, thinking aloud. Carl's eyes twinkled and he pulled her close. She'd wanted him to respond with something wonderfully romantic but he just smiled. From then on they'd spent lazy days down on the beach. She'd happily let Carl go off on his own a few times to explore the craggy coastline, leaving her on the beach. Her pale olive skin tanned easily and after four days she looked and felt great. Carl had kept a tight hold of her in the bars during the long evenings, although he hadn't been short of admiring glances himself. He'd smiled a lot those two weeks. She felt they could go anywhere and find whatever they needed in each other, it had been a wonderful feeling. The only thing she would have changed was feeling too exhausted at the end of the two weeks to go out and ending up spending the last few evenings apart from him.

The photographs had been fantastic, the best one had been taken of them both by the beach bar man. Jenna had never seen a better photo of herself – petite beside Carl, her hair looking a little wild from the sun and sea. It had all been so wonderful and romantic.

Jenna had never visited Carl at university. She hadn't met James and Mark or the girls Carl had mentioned occasionally, Sarah and some brunette called Maxine. She had wanted to go for a weekend but he had discouraged it.

"I like to come home to see you, don't want any of my mates taking you away."

Carl had been back twice over the winter term. He'd been quiet, but Jenna was content – until just after he had returned for the Christmas holidays and spoken the words that struck like a steel dagger into her heart:

"Maybe we should cool it for a while. You know, with me being away."

Suddenly the blue eyes were distant, his tone unfamiliar.

"It's nothing you've done. I just have a lot of work and it's all getting too much with exams soon. I need a break." Carl didn't look at her. The words were so impersonally spoken. He could have been talking to anyone. She had stared at him, unbelieving.

"Why? You had work last year and it was no problem! What's going on? Tell me!"

"There's no problem," he said quickly. "Sorry Jenna. I just need some space." Then he went. After two years that was all he left her with and Christmas was rotten. She'd rung and rung his house for some answers after the initial shock, but he had gone away for Christmas and New Year.

The following first week of January, when Jenna had decided he must be back home was when she had seen the girl, a tall brunette. Jenna knew that Carl was in the house on his own, his dad was away. She watched the girl walk down the path and shut the small gate. The latch rattled in its distinctive way. Was *she* the reason? Jenna hadn't felt up to screaming at anyone in the street, she was too shocked. She'd have preferred not to, but she remembered the girl's face, aquiline features and dark eyes, the heavy eyeliner.

He had left her tortured and shocked, still haunted by the "Whys?" What had she done wrong? What hadn't she done? She couldn't move her life on until she knew. And now she had run away to a place which lived, breathed and smelt of him, and when she actually concentrated on her surroundings, their desolation in comparison to the summer appeared to mirror her feelings exactly.

Her mum had said that if she *had* to go back, then she must think about the future and forget about Carl. Jenna was thinking about the future – but forget about Carl? She felt as if his features had been etched across her mind's eye. His face was waiting around the corners as she wandered the paved streets, his image hidden in every vacant stare – lean, strong jawed and touched by a golden tan. The tight feeling in her stomach wouldn't go away – it had taken hold.

After two years, his deep-set blue eyes had still caused her to gasp silently. Jenna knew she was the envy of many girls back home and she didn't blame them. She just missed him. Since returning to Majorca she'd spent hours thinking about the many times they had sat on a bus together or watched a video in silence and Jenna wished she had made more of those times, that they had talked. She didn't want to think she had wasted a single minute.

Now back on the island, she was sitting watching the same sea, churned up, weed strewn and set against a bleak winter sky. It had been two days since she'd stepped off the bus that wound its way across the island from Palma. Two days of sitting around, alone in the cafés with a single cup of coffee. On one occasion she had almost ordered two cups to imagine Carl was sitting opposite her. When she realized what a stupid idea it was she had cried. She'd spent most of the time staring blankly and thinking about the huge contrasts. Then and now. With him and without.

A gust of wind from the sea suddenly whipped her long hair, the colour of brass, off her shoulders. She looked a tiny, forlorn figure against the expanse of the bay, dressed simply in a silver-grey jogging top, deep blue denim jeans and suede trainers. Jenna slapped her hands down on her thighs and pulled herself up from the weather-beaten bar bench where she had spent the last two hours, squinting her amber eyes and dark eyebrows, wide and slightly arched, against the gale blowing through the bay.

Back in September the beach bar set into the rock at the back of the beach had been the hub of the bay, now it was unmanned and desolate, its tables stacked and chained under the canopy. Jenna had been watching the ferocious waves, but she felt detached from the whole scene, her thoughts far away from its reality. She had come back expecting to relive the dream of the two of them together, but the happy feelings were long gone and she now knew that they couldn't be conjured up by her reckless return. I should have gone and sat in the local park to sort myself out, she thought. At least it would have been cheaper.

She ran a hand through a section of hair that the wind blew across her eye and pulled up the hood of the zip-up top to protect her small, pretty features from the biting wind.

"Time for lunch," Jenna spoke aloud. She had got used to two things since arriving – not having a clue what time it was and talking to herself. By returning, she felt as though she was intruding on the locals' winter respite from the rowdy foreigners who besieged the small village in the summertime. These winter months were when they claimed their home back, when the fishermen could drag their boats up and down an empty beach and the bar owners could entertain their friends in the quiet corners of their vine-covered premises. They were all going about their own business at their own pace.

There was a sudden blast of sharp wind and Jenna's attention was caught by activity up in the wooden fish restaurant. It was an old shack-like construction built on a natural plateau halfway up the tall light brown rock which formed the left-hand side of the bay. Jenna had climbed the steps to it a couple of times during the summer for refreshment when the beach bar was too busy. Its cool interior had provided a great view of the sun-kissed bay. In September, Carl had stayed on the beach sunning himself, sending Jenna on errands to the bar and up to the restaurant. She didn't mind, she enjoyed doing anything for him.

Now, she wanted to eat. It was a twenty-minute walk back up to the village main street and the shack seemed open for business, unlike the previous two days, so Jenna crossed the shale to the bottom of the steps that were carved into the rock face. As she ascended, the raw sound of the waves pummelling the pebbles and dragging the top layer backwards became more distant, almost tranquil.

You never came up here with me, Jenna remembered as she reached the shack. The thought cheered her. She had found a place away from Carl.

She ordered fish in broken Spanish from the friendly, large Majorcan woman behind the wooden counter, who seemed to be managing the whole show on her own. Jenna settled at a table in the far corner of the hut overlooking the beach. There was only a flimsy wooden railing between her chair and the crumbly-looking rock below, which descended into the angry waves. She thought about the holiday photo of them. They looked so perfect together. Jenna formed her mouth into a tight smile to stop the tears from falling. She wished they could be happy and together like that always.

The sudden eruption of sizzling hot oil brought Jenna back from her recollections. A lively discussion in Spanish reached her ears from the kitchen alcove behind the counter, between the friendly woman who had served Jenna and someone else hidden from her view. Jenna watched the woman's open face, she was smiling, listening to the male voice, waiting to laugh with the two customers sitting at the near table, locals, Jenna presumed. The scene was enough to bring a smile to her face.

She looked back to the bay as a chorus of laughter erupted. The waves still crashed in. The booming followed by water dragging at the shale provided an almost hypnotic background. Jenna felt like a seabird on its rocky perch, spying on the scene below. She could now see the source of amusement in the kitchen, a man with jet black hair stood with his back to the restaurant, busying himself behind the counter.

"*Aqui tiene, Senorita.*"

The woman was at her table. She smiled and placed the food and wrapped cutlery on the table. It looked wonderful. Jenna had never tasted anything as good as the simplicity of the pure white flakes of fish. As she ate, two other sets of people entered the shack and the cooking alcove had become a hive of sizzling oil and steam. She glanced over to the counter. A young Majorcan man was polishing glasses, the jet black locks which fell across his forehead trembled as he completed the job with care, his brow furrowed, dark eyes squinting.

She watched him place the thoroughly dried glass down on the counter and glance out into the restaurant, catching her now unguarded inquisitive gaze. His face relaxed and he smiled across at her, briefly, almost hesitantly. Jenna blinked, feeling embarrassed at being caught practically gawping, especially as the subject was rather lovely. She awkwardly returned the gesture before stabbing at the remains of her food.

She watched the waves, concentrating on matching their movement to the boom and dragging sound. There was nothing going on in the bay but Jenna had never been someone who was easily bored. She sat and watched as the early customers drifted back down the steps. Now she was watching and thinking, trying desperately to watch without thinking about Carl and missing him.

Over by the kitchen the smiling lady appeared to have gone. Jenna and the two other diners were the only customers remaining – plus the man behind the counter with his back to her. Jenna caught his eye again as he turned. He half nodded before moving purposefully around the counter and approaching her table. She looked up at the stranger cautiously, taking in the jet black jeans and fitted black T-shirt.

He spoke in English.

"I am having a coffee now I am finished, would you like one also?"

His voice was gravelly and mature for his age, twenty-five-ish, she guessed. The question had been put to her almost nervously. The dark eyes waited for her response. No cocky look or silly grin. The expression was serious, yet soft.

Jenna heard herself reply.

"Yes... Thank you."

He was away swiftly back to the counter. Heavy black boots sounded strong footsteps on the wooden floor as he retreated. He returned almost immediately with two cups and settled himself opposite her, spending rather too long shuffling the chair into a satisfactory position.

The stranger finally looked up and nodded at Jenna.

"I like to watch the sea too and I saw you looking from over there," he indicated over his shoulder to the counter. "Is fantastic, eh? when the sea is angry, like this."

He looked right into her eyes as he spoke with great intensity, but his expression put her at ease. His hair curled around his ears in heavy locks, strong eyebrows framed dark brown eyes. Jenna was aware that she was smiling across the table. She liked the strong stereotypical Spanish accent.

"My name is Javier," he announced dramatically with a nervously flashed smile. Jenna wasn't prepared for conversation but tried to respond to the friendly stranger.

"I'm Jenna … thanks for the coffee. Do you own the restaurant?"

"No… *Si*, well, er, it belongs to my family. You like our food?"

"It was beautiful, very nice."

"*Bueno*, my mother fried the fish." He smiled again, friendly and sincere. "You are English?"

Jenna nodded and there was a pause as both of them looked down into the waves.

"My English is no so good," he went on apologetically. "I would like to speak it as you do."

"But your accent is nice," Jenna replied honestly. "I like hearing Spanish accents on TV or in films."

His expression lit up. "You like the cinema? Me too."

Jenna tried to cool down the rapport she had struck with the stranger. "Are you open all winter? I didn't think I saw anyone up here yesterday."

"No. We open today for two weeks, special time, we are having the surfing competition, many people will come." He was serious again.

Jenna shot him an expression of mock alarm and gestured down to the water.

"People will surf in that?"

"Yes! Was my idea." Javier nodded enthusiastically then looked down at his coffee, his nervous enthusiasm for the conversation seemed to have suddenly evaporated.

"Three years ago, my friend, Emilio, he died in the water."

The revelation shook Jenna. "I'm sorry."

"Is OK ... he died surfing when the black flag was flying. Nobody was here at the beach." Javier looked across the table at Jenna.

"I still don't know how he died, but the sea

... it was too much for him, I think..." He closed his mouth tightly and peered at the waves for a couple of seconds before turning back to Jenna. He smiled.

"So! I decided with my brothers to start a winter surfing week, our friends who are lifeguards in Soller will come to help, to see for danger. We only surf on a red flag, never black, never," he finished firmly.

"It's a nice way to remember your friend," Jenna said gently.

"I think so. Me and others here, we miss Emilio. He was a good friend, since I was two I knew him ... all the girls liked him," Javier added with a grin. He had spoken in a strong, sure tone, with measured emotion at the memory of his friend. Jenna felt the sadness of the story. She stared at her coffee and allowed her mind to ponder the details.

"We own another bar in the Village, Sergio's – where I work all summer. Do you know it?"

Jenna nodded.

"I remember it from the summer but I didn't go in there. I was here in September ... on holiday."

"Then why do you come back here now?" he asked slowly.

His eyes fell down to the table awkwardly on noting her reaction to the question. He had sat down to talk, made no attempt at cheesy flattery, he was just nice. She noted how lovely he looked sitting opposite her, staring down at the sea. His soft manner was a revelation considering his looks. Jenna had listened to his sad story – it had involved her. She realized that in the five brief minutes of conversation she had not thought about Carl. Suddenly she wanted to tell Javier about why she was back. After all, telling people she knew had done her no good.

"It's OK. I don't mind you asking. You're right. It is strange that I'm back here now and I came back on my own for a special reason." She started speaking, staring vacantly at the table, knowing Javier was listening.

"When I was here in September I was with someone, Carl..."

It took her five minutes to convey the holiday, the two years with Carl, the nightmare at Christmas, the girl in the street, the not knowing. She spoke with a sad smile and wide-eyed expression, as if relaying a distant memory.

"...so I'm back here. It was supposed to help me, make me focus on the future and sort myself out. But seeing all the places where we walked, the beach..." she trailed off.

"I feel like that when I look at the sea about my friend ... when I saw you looking at the water, I could see that you had sadness in your eyes. I hope it is better now, Jenna ... that you told me."

Jenna liked the way he said her name. She grasped her wallet which lay on the table and opened it out.

"This is Carl." She turned the wallet around to show him the bland passport photo, taken shortly before they left.

He glanced interestedly at it. Jenna saw the flash of recognition alter his expression as a shout came from the counter.

"Javier! *Puedes ayudarme?*"

The man had a look of Javier, but older, harsher and more stockily built. Jenna withdrew her wallet and Javier placed a hand gently on her arm.

"Jenna, I must be going with my brother to Soller now. Will you come here again tomorrow? I liked to talk to you." She detected the request in his statement. He looked hassled and his expression was once more intense.

"I see you tomorrow. OK?" He waited for a response. Jenna smiled with her eyes and nodded slowly.

"I'll come down around lunchtime."

Javier closed and padlocked the slatted gate behind them.

"I must go, goodbye." Jenna watched him hurriedly descend the flat steps to join his brother down on the beach. They walked up the road to the small dusty car park where they climbed into a silver van and drove away.

Jenna thought about Javier. He was so far from the stereotype local. His eyes were captivating, liquid brown, his mouth full, kind. Jenna liked the intensity of his expression and the cautiousness of his approach.

She headed back to the village. Her hair streamed behind her as the wind rushed through the passage that the road carved through the high rocks on either side of the valley.

He had seen Carl before, the previous September. But there was more than just recognizing the face. Javier knew something that Jenna did not, she was sure of it and afraid. The gnawing feeling of loss in her stomach was replaced by a sense of dread.

Walking back to the hotel she began to feel less conspicuous as an outsider. Deya was by no means busy, but a few more people occupied the tables in the café-bar on the right and further up, through the white archway to Sergio's, the stools at the bar were all in use.

It was around two o'clock the following day when Jenna rounded the last bend in the winding road. She had taken her time to wander down to the bay. Pacing herself, preparing for what she might learn, refusing to entertain certain options. The wind had been less raw during the walk and the gap in the cliffs marking the entrance to the beach revealed a calmer sea and the red flag flying high from the railings of the shack.

Jenna felt an involuntary fizz of excitement as she glanced up at the restaurant. She had already eaten. Javier was behind the bar when she reached the top of the steps, again in black, polishing glasses, concentration again etched across his face.

When he saw Jenna he looked surprised and happy – gesturing her to take a stool at the counter.

"Is late, I thought you would not come," he said light-heartedly.

She settled on the stool as he began frothing milk in a silver jug. He placed two cups under the dual spouts of the coffee machine. Behind him in the alcove his mother cooked, swathed in a cloud of steam. She looked around at the sound of voices and smiled at Jenna.

"How are you today?" Javier inquired, placing the coffee in front of her.

"OK." Her tone was positive. *Don't beat about the bush,* she told herself. *You're here now. Find out.*

"When I showed you that photograph yesterday..." She began firmly but couldn't maintain it. "You've seen him before, haven't you... Carl? You remember him from the summer."

Javier finished with the chocolate powder shaker and placed it down slowly. He stared out into the restaurant for a moment and then sighed.

"I was thinking about you last night, Jenna ... if I were you, what would be for the best … for me to tell you. I think you feel very sad … and what I say, will not make it many times…" He paused, struggling to find the word. "*Peor* … worse?"

Javier took a deep breath and looked into her eyes.

"I remember your man, Jenna, from Sergio's. But when I speak to him you were no there." Javier's dark eyes and strong eyebrows framed his expression of sincerity.

"Well I *must* have been there!" Jenna responded quickly. She was afraid now.

"Jenna, really. I don't know why you were not there, but you were not. You say you never went to Sergio's. It was a busy night, the night of the fireworks?"

"What fireworks?" She frantically scoured her memory, then remembered the two evenings at the end of the stay that she had spent in the room, feeling tired – wanting to spend the last evenings with Carl, away from the crazy atmosphere in the bars. He had gone out and insisted she remained in the room to rest. His "half hour" out had turned out to be the whole evening each time. Lying in the room she had heard the distant sound of voices from the bars and the muffled explosions.

"I stayed in that night."

"Do you remember now?" he asked, watching her. Jenna nodded, eyes glazed.

"I want you to know, so I tell you. Your Carl, he was with a girl." Jenna's stomach twisted. It was one of the options she had refuted. She wished Javier would vanish.

"What girl... What do you mean?" Her voice was shaky.

"He was with a girl for two nights in the bar, I saw them, Emilio saw them. He remember him too."

Jenna's amber eyes flashed.

"How do you know it was Carl?" she demanded angrily. "There must have been hundreds of different people there."

"I remember his face..." Javier began to sound helpless.

"Why him? Why do you remember him, Javier?"

Javier sighed. "Because he was drunk and he tried to punch me when I tell him, so I remember him, OK! And then I see him again in your picture. Is true, I'm sorry ... it is!" he finished, rattled and grave-faced.

Jenna didn't know what she was staring at because it was a blur. Her head spun as she tried to absorb what Javier had just revealed. A total blankness struck her thoughts, the sound of the other diners in the shack faded away to a single background tone. She felt as though she had been dealt a blow to the head and she was in limbo, between feeling the pain and falling down.

Someone had taken hold of her arm, had clasped their fingers around it. It felt warm and then hot. Jenna moved from the stool and out of the shack. She descended the steps, her right arm extended and her hand brushing against the rock to steady herself. Tears streamed down her face.

She didn't know where she was going until she sat down on the bench under the canopy of the beach bar. She believed Javier, the reaction in his face to the photograph in the wallet was too certain to deny.

"Come with me to Sergio's." The gentle voice came from beside her on the bench. Javier leaned towards her and placed a hand on her shoulder, so gently she could hardly feel it.

"I am sorry I make you cry," he said. The look in his dark eyes was full of compassion.

"Come with me. I will show you something."

He stood up, the glossy tendrils of his hair teased his eyelashes as he looked down at Jenna. She took the hand which was extended towards her, warm and strong. Once she was standing it was released.

He walked slightly ahead of her, leading her across the shale until they reached the tarmacked road. Jenna walked beside him, drawing her jogging top closely around her, feeling cold. She hugged herself and wished Javier had not let go of her hand.

As they wound their way up the valley, the sun shone with surprising strength, bathing the olive groves on either side of the road. Jenna watched only the grey concrete rushing under her footsteps as she walked, occasionally raising a hand to brush away silent tears.

The road gave way to the paved narrow streets and they reached Sergio's. No one sat at the bar, unlike the day before. Javier took a seat at the far end and pulled it out for Jenna, before taking the one next to it.

"I will show you who she was. You should see."

Behind him, Jenna noticed the large clip-frame protecting a scattering of flash photographs, showing the dark background of the bar at night and bronzed, smiling faces.

"This is her." Javier was pointing to a thin face, mouth smiling widely responding to the camera lens. She moved forward to see the face more clearly. Dark hair, high cheekbones and a straight nose. Dark eyes, heavy eyeliner. A match. The brunette from the street. Jenna recalled the vision of the girl closing the rattling gate and walking down the pavement towards her. Those same eyes.

"Her name was Maxine. She was with your Carl."

Maxine. The name had come to her from Carl's lips – one of the crowd she had never met. Jenna rested her forehead in her hand, mentally counting all the "whys" which had been obliterated by the last hour's revelations. She looked at Javier and for a second wondered if he was real. He'd been a genie-like voice of the truth. Had she dreamt him up? Wonderfully shy, sexy voice, good body, taking an interest in her, telling her what she did and didn't want to know.

"I no like her, Maxine. She had, how you

say... 'gleeter'? in the hair ... cheap ... and she went with my brother. She say to Emilio she study at university but she had bad manners. I show you her because I want to tell you all I know ... and you to see how different she is to you." Jenna couldn't raise her face to his. She looked at the darkly lined eyes once more.

"I've seen her at home, near Carl's house."

"They knew each other from before, I sure. After she went with Emilio we watch her, in here. We see her and your man meet and talk – they laugh a lot – and we see them again the night after, together and drink much."

Jenna didn't want to hear any more. It was all too much now. As she closed her eyes several tears brimmed over in quick succession and fell on to the bar. Her shoulders trembled as she let the despair flow out. She felt betrayed and stupid in thinking the holiday had been so romantic. It all seemed so sinister now. She thought about the suddenness of the arrangements. The feeling she'd felt, but quickly dismissed that Carl was expecting her not to be able to afford the trip, all the times he had gone off on his own "exploring", making her stay on the beach when she was happy to accompany him. He hadn't wanted her there, she could see it all so clearly now.

Javier placed his hand over Jenna's small one and rested it there for a long while. It felt warm and strong. When she brushed the tears away from her delicate features for the final time and attempted an expression of composure, Javier placed his arm around her shoulder and peered into her face. She exhaled deeply and raised her head.

"I'm OK now."

He looked at her disbelievingly.

"I know you are, how you say, upset? but Jenna, is better to be angry – in silence. Sad makes you look behind, angry is better for going forward. He was bad to you, a villain!"

Jenna listened to the words. They made sense.

"If he wants the other lady, then he has lost you. You no want him back, Jenna. Carl has done very bad to you. *Es un... un...*" Javier flicked his head theatrically and banged a fist down on the bar instead of finishing the sentence.

He took a deep breath, as he had done in

the shack before he spoke earlier, it seemed ages ago to Jenna.

"I also see you, Jenna, in September, the one night I was no working in here, I go to Jaime's to see my friend, he work there. I see you with Carl." Jenna suddenly looked at him wide-eyed.

"I was in the back room talking with Jose and looking into the bar. I see your Carl tell you to buy a drink when the bar was with many people, but you do not go quickly. Then he make like this..." Javier pulled an unpleasantly aggressive frown.

"...and he say something and then you go."

Jenna managed a laugh at this snatched memory.

"Carl was like that, he got moody if he didn't get his own way."

Javier was looking back at her in disbelief.

"He talk like that *many* times?"

Yes he did, Jenna suddenly thought to herself.

"He didn't mean anything..."

Of course he didn't mean anything. Jenna had got used to the feeling when he snapped at her, sneered when she didn't do something immediately. It was like he was speaking to some kind of public official who had irritated him. She just accepted that that was Carl, that was how he was. Javier was right though, she shouldn't have accepted it. His look of surprise when she revealed that the scene in the bar was Carl's usual manner had jolted her – the outsider's view.

"What are you thinking now?" Javier asked, his voice gentle and deep. He said the words like she would expect to hear them from a lover.

"I'm thinking about what you said. I'm kind of seeing it all from a different view. I feel different. What were you going to call him? You sounded good speaking Spanish with anger."

Javier smirked sexily and brushed his hair slowly up away from his forehead. "Is no for a lady to hear, Jenna." He sighed. "Will you come here tonight again? We open to start the surfing festival. You can come and sit and watch, talk to me. I think maybe you enjoy it."

As Jenna wandered back to the hotel at the end of the street she thought it felt warmer. She had stayed in the bar drinking coffee with Javier until it closed for an hour to allow them to prepare for the evening. They had talked about themselves, listened intently to all the basic details usually exchanged as a mundane duty.

Jenna thought of Carl as she walked. No one at home had questioned his behaviour or had the licence to lay into him. She felt better being angry, with Carl as the "villain". The wonderful romantic break had been something else altogether for Carl. Jenna couldn't be bothered to wonder about Maxine, with the "gleeter" in her hair – she didn't care about her.

"He's lost *me*! Now that *is* a good one." Jenna was looking forward to the evening. She felt oddly cleansed, not totally, but she had been distracted. Nothing at home had managed to do that. The nagging ache in her stomach had lost its grip.

Jenna entered the news shop just before the hotel and flicked through a copy of Spanish *Vogue*. The new season's citric colours leapt from the page. They looked fantastic on the catwalk against the models' tanned limbs. Next door in the beach shop she bought a vibrant blue V-neck T-shirt.

"I'll come and sit and watch, then," she

had told Javier. She'd be happy to do that if the rest of the bar was empty! A bemused smile crept across her face and she was happy to let it stay there.

Four days left. Time to concentrate on other things, perhaps.

Magic Carpet

Lorna Read

It was the Christmas holidays and Ceri was helping her father in his clothes shop. Normally, she thoroughly enjoyed it, but not this time. Instead of cheerfully greeting customers and asking if she could help them, she hid away in the stockroom for as long as she possibly could, feeling utterly listless and sick at heart.

She couldn't even summon up any enthusiasm about Christmas itself. Last Christmas David had given her the best present she'd ever had. He'd bought her a spaniel puppy, black and white and bouncy and licky.

Ceri had named him Dumbo because of his enormous ears, and he slept in her bedroom at night and was her constant companion. A lot more constant than David had turned out to be. He had finished with her in the summer and it had been Dumbo who had helped her get over her broken heart with his unfailing affection and devotion. But in November Dumbo had slipped his collar, rushed out into the road and been knocked over by a van. Ceri had rushed after him, calling his name, but it was too late. She'd knelt in the middle of the road, cradling his bloodstained head, shedding bitter tears over his poor, broken body, ignoring the impatient traffic hooting all around her.

It had been a terrible experience and, after five weeks, she still felt as battered as Dumbo's poor little body had been. She felt frozen inside and didn't think she was capable of loving any creature, two-legged or four-legged, ever again.

A loud rapping on the door of the stockroom roused her from her tearful memories.

"Ceri? Ceri, you must have finished checking off that jeans delivery by now. It's Julie's lunchtime, you're needed in the shop," her father called.

Reluctantly, Ceri left her safe haven and tried to force a smile on to her drooping features.

"Cheer up, love," her father said. "I've got some news that might make you feel better. I've been sent some samples of cotton goods from Turkey and I'm thinking of making a trip to Istanbul in the New Year. Fancy coming with me?"

"What about Mum? Won't she want to go?" Ceri asked.

"You know Mum. She hates flying. Anyway, we both thought it would be a change for you. The weather won't be any better than here in Colwyn Bay, but at least there are lots of new things to see."

Which was how, on January 4th, Ceri came to be studying a guidebook in mid-air while her father sat beside her, poring over piles of paperwork. Somehow, though, she found she was unable to concentrate on the page she was trying to read. It wasn't the noise and vibration of the plane, it wasn't even the constant interruptions from stewardesses. She didn't know what it was.

She sighed and looked up from her book. Her father was making pencil scribbles in the margin of a computer printout. An air hostess asked if she would like a drink and she ordered a orange juice. The drinks trolley moved on – and immediately Ceri located the source of her disturbance. One row back from hers, across the aisle, sat a boy, an extremely good-looking blond-haired boy, and he was staring right at her.

She gave a little jump as her eyes met his, then quickly looked away again and back to her book. After a few moments, she sneaked a quick glance and there he was, still looking at her.

She felt herself blush and, in her confusion, her hand wobbled, splashing her father's papers with bright orange.

"Sorry, Dad!" she said.

He then spent the next half hour telling her all about the import–export business and when she next had a chance to look round, the boy had closed his eyes and gone to sleep.

When the plane landed, her father spent ages looking for something he'd dropped on the floor. They were the last people to leave the plane and she didn't see the boy again. But her disappointment quickly evaporated in the excitement of being in Istanbul.

A half-hour taxi ride took them to their hotel, the Grand Yavus. As they settled down to a meal in the hotel restaurant, Ceri's father laid the ground rules for the holiday.

"This is a Muslim country and it's very different from Britain. Here, girls do *not* walk round the streets on their own," he said. "It's simply not done. It's asking for trouble. The tour buses will pick you up at the hotel and drop you back again. If you're not on a tour or with me, you must stay here in the hotel. I won't think of you going out alone, it's far too dangerous."

Ceri promised she wouldn't. In fact, his words had filled her with terror. Kidnappers, drug runners, the white slave trade...

"I've got a meeting in the morning so I've booked you on a tour of Topkapi Palace," her father continued. "A minibus will collect you at nine-thirty and bring you back at one. I'll be back by then, so we'll have lunch together and go out in the afternoon, OK?"

Ceri's reply was to let out a loud yawn. "Sorry, Dad," she apologized, "I think I'd better get to bed."

She took the lift up to her room on the third floor. Before she settled down to sleep, she opened the balcony door and gazed out at the lighted windows of the town and the tiny, twinkling, star-like lamps on the myriad boats moored on the Straits of Bosphorus.

She inhaled a deep draught of smoky night air and felt a thrilled tingle shoot all over the surface of her skin. She was so far away from home, in such an alien place. It was incredibly exciting. Suddenly, she thought of the boy on the plane. What was he doing now? Was he standing on a balcony looking out at the Bosphorus, too?

She shook her head wistfully. "No use dreaming," she told herself. "He's gone. And anyway, you're off men. Remember David..."

The emeralds in the Topkapi Palace Treasury were as large as a man's clenched fist and glittered brilliantly in the harsh spotlights. Ceri's nose touched the glass case as she marvelled at the vast wealth of the sultans who had once owned such incredible jewels. In the next showcase was the famous emerald-studded gold dagger, which appeared in the film, *Topkapi*. She was gazing at it when a male voice said, "Hello".

Ceri spun round, about to glare at whoever was daring to try and pick her up, but found herself smiling instead. It was the boy from the plane – tall, dressed in dark grey jeans and a brown padded leather jacket, his blond hair gleaming in the Treasury's bright lights.

"I saw you on the plane yesterday," he said.

"That's right," she replied. "I remember."

"What a coincidence, running into you like this! Isn't the palace amazing?" he said. "I just can't believe that people used to live in places as big as this. You could fit my flat four times into this one room! My name's Paul, by the way."

"I'm Ceri."

"Where's the man you were with on the plane?" asked Paul.

"You mean my dad? He's at a business meeting," she explained.

"Oh, so it was your father! That's a relief. I thought you went in for much older men!" Paul joked.

"Is that why you didn't say anything to me?" Ceri asked.

"Well ... yes!" Paul admitted. "I was dying to chat you up but didn't relish a slap round the head from a jealous husband!"

Ceri laughed. "Have you seen everything else?" she asked him.

"All except the Harem."

"Me too. I think that's my group over there, waiting to go in."

"It looks like my lot's going in, too. Stick by me and I'll make sure nobody sells you to a sultan," Paul joked.

They walked down long, cobble-stoned corridors and into cold stone rooms with marble floors and ornate stained-glass windows.

"Brrr," Ceri rubbed her gloved hands together. "I can see the point of all this marble for keeping cool in summer, but whatever did they do in winter?"

"They had wood-burning stoves and they put carpets everywhere, even on the walls to keep away draughts. They wore heavy clothes in winter, you know, furs and sheepskin and thick velvet. They didn't always trip around in seven veils," Paul said.

"You know a lot about it," she remarked.

"And so I should. I'm studying Middle Eastern art and architecture at Manchester. I'm in my second year. How about you?"

Ceri told him about the A-level courses she was taking. He didn't seem to mind that she was still at school. The two year age gap didn't really matter. She marvelled at how easy he was to talk to. It was as if they had known each other for ages.

A fizzy, excited feeling started bubbling away inside her. *Stop it*, she told herself. *Remember David. He broke your heart. You vowed never to go out with anyone else.*

But David was five whole months in the

past. Perhaps her heart was recovering – as far as boys were concerned, that was. Dogs were another matter...

All too soon they found themselves out in the bare gardens. It was a grey day with a biting wind. Sleet was starting to fall.

"I've got to get my minibus back to my hotel now. I'm meeting Dad for lunch," Ceri said. She hesitated. "It's been nice..."

She felt her words – and maybe her hopes, too – trail away into nothing and she cursed her over-active imagination. *I expect this is it*, she thought sadly. *He'll say goodbye and I'll never see him again. He probably doesn't fancy me, anyway. He's probably just being friendly. He saw me on my own and felt sorry for me. Just my luck!*

She felt her smile fade and the corners of her mouth droop as if pulled down by invisible magnets.

Then, out of the blue, he asked, "What are you doing later? Have you and your dad got any plans, or will he let me whisk you away for a Turkish pizza?"

Ceri felt breathless. And tingly. And indescribably happy.

"Dad hasn't mentioned anything," she said. "I'll ask him at lunchtime."

"And I'll drop by your hotel at about seven-thirty and hope you'll be there," Paul said. "I'm staying not far from you. I'm in a students' hostel by the old Turkish baths. It's a bit grotty. Till seven-thirty, then!"

He gave her a look and a smile that made her feel as if she were being whizzed upwards in an express lift.

"I'll be there," she promised. "See you!"

"Well…" her father said when she told him. "I'm a bit worried about letting you loose in Istanbul with a total stranger."

"He's a perfectly normal boy," Ceri assured him. "See him for yourself and make your own mind up." She was crossing her fingers beneath the wooden table in a restaurant quaintly named The Pudding Shop.

"I shall," her father said, "and if I approve of him – and I only said 'if', mind! – then he can take you out on strict instructions that he'll get you back by eleven-thirty and that I know exactly where you're going."

Paul walked in on the dot of seven-thirty, just as Ceri and her father were changing some traveller's cheques into Turkish lira at the reception desk. Ceri introduced the two of them. At first, the conversation was restricted to questions about which hotel

Paul was staying at, and where he lived in England. Paul actually showed her father his passport, which Ceri thought was going a bit too far. But she knew it was all in a good cause and that he was trying to prove that he was who he said he was.

She realized Paul had her father's approval when her dad asked, "So which restaurant are you going to, then?"

"I don't know what it's called, but it's just on the right at the top of the street and has a man in Turkish costume standing in the doorway. I walked past it on my way back from the Blue Mosque this afternoon and thought it looked fun," Paul said.

"Have a good time, and make sure Ceri's back by eleven-thirty or I'll start to worry," Mr Williams said.

"He's nice, your dad," Paul remarked as they walked up steep Piyer Loti street towards the main road. "You've got to forgive him for being anxious. It just shows how much he cares."

And you're nice, too, for thinking that, thought Ceri, and promptly stumbled over a broken paving stone.

"Careful," said Paul, taking hold of her elbow. He kept his hand there and it was like a burning presence which Ceri could feel right through her jacket.

When they came out into the brightly lit main road of Divan Yolu, he took his hand away and Ceri felt its absence. She felt like a small boat adrift, its mooring rope cut.

"Here we are," Paul said, stopping outside the restaurant.

The doorman in the red fez bowed them in and called a waiter, who showed them to a low, circular table at which they sat on large cushions.

Their waiter explained that if they ordered *meze*, they would be able to try a bit of everything. When she thought about it later, back in her hotel room, Ceri thought she would remember the taste, look and smell of every one of those exotic foods for the rest of her days – all her senses seemed so much sharper than usual. It was being in Paul's presence that had done it. He made her aware of every tiny thing – the chink of one saucer against another, the tang of the hot, red chilli sauce, the slippery bitterness of an olive against the tip of her tongue.

As she ate, Ceri watched Paul as he talked. He had a mobile face on which different expressions chased themselves like cloud shadows across a Welsh hillside. There was never a gap in their conversation, unlike with David, where Ceri had often found herself struggling to think of things to say to him.

When, at last, they had eaten as much as they could, and ordered a last round of fragrant Turkish tea to wash it down, the waiter brought them a saucer of Turkish Delight and some wooden sticks like toothpicks to eat it with.

Paul speared a squidgy pink square. As he lifted it into the air, a powdery cloud of icing sugar dropped from it. He leant towards Ceri, offering the sweet marshmallow to her mouth. She licked her lips and parted them and allowed him to push the sweet gently between them. She laughed. Icing sugar got up her nose and she sneezed and spluttered. Her eyes watered and she couldn't stop giggling and sniffing as the Turkish Delight melted in her mouth.

"Here," Paul said, offering her a paper napkin. "You've got a white moustache!"

If she had been with any other new date she had been trying to impress, the knowledge that her face was covered in white powder would have mortified her. But with Paul, it didn't matter. It was all part of the fun time they were having.

"It's lovely," she said, meaning the Turkish Delight.

"So are you, Ceri."

She stared at him, feeling everything suddenly stand still – time, other people, her own heartbeat. "Oh, come on!" she scoffed. "I've got my grandma's bumpy nose and look at this hair, it's impossible!"

"I think it's a very pretty nose," Paul said. "Sort of aristocratic."

Ceri stared at him. "Nobody's ever called my nose that before." She gave a nervous chuckle. Was he having her on, or did he mean it?

"Look at *my* nose," he said. "I broke it playing football when I was twelve. Now that's what *I* call a bump!"

She smiled as he tapped the slightly crooked bridge of his nose, thinking it made him look even more handsome.

Paul walked her back to her hotel and just as the uniformed doorman was about to open the door for her, he pulled her gently to one side, into the shadows.

"Let me kiss that bumpy nose," he said and the next second, she felt the soft touch of his warm lips on the tip of her nose. It tickled but it was wonderful. And then he kissed her on her forehead, on both cheeks, and finally on her mouth, a gentle kiss which didn't last long, but lingered just long enough to leave her dying for more.

"Thanks for coming out with me tonight. It was a great evening," he said. "What are you doing tomorrow?"

"I don't know yet," Ceri said.

"I'm going to the university library in the morning, but I'll be free after lunch. Do you fancy going round the Grand Bazaar?"

"I'd love to," Ceri said. "I've seen it on television and it looked fantastic. I need to find a present for Mum. I don't want to leave it till the last day. Oh, I wish I wasn't going home on Thursday. I've only got one more night. You're so lucky having a whole week..."

"I wish you weren't going home as well! What time's your flight?" asked Paul.

"Seven o'clock in the evening. We have to check in at five."

"It's not so bad, then. At least we've got two more whole days."

Ceri loved the way he said "we". It meant he was thinking of them as a pair, Ceri and Paul, Paul and Ceri. It sounded equally good whichever way you said it.

"Meet you here at two o'clock, then. And Ceri…"

His voice became softer, deeper, and a thrill ran right through her as she waited.

His lips approached her again, met her lips and their mouths pressed together. One stinging, piercing moment of passion then his lips left hers again and she stood there breathless, her legs weak.

"…I'm so glad you were on my plane," he said.

In the morning, Ceri and her father went round the Blue Mosque. It wasn't blue outside, it was a kind of dirty grey, but its name came from all the shades of blue in its tiles and stained-glass windows.

He had another meeting that afternoon, so he was pleased that Paul had offered to take her to the bazaar. After lunch, he took her back to the door of the hotel, then hailed a passing taxi, telling Ceri to meet him back at the hotel at six-thirty.

As soon as she got through the hotel doors, Ceri saw a familiar figure sitting in one of the black leather armchairs in the foyer. Paul leapt to his feet and held out his hands to her and she took them, loving the firm grip of his fingers around hers. He kept her hand in his as they walked up the hill to the main road and past the old Turkish baths, until a small sidestreet, crowded with shoppers, indicated one of the many rabbit-hole-like entrances to the bazaar.

"Oh, wow! So much gold!" Ceri exclaimed as they entered the fringes of the bazaar where the jewellers had their glittering shops.

They strolled along for a while, admiring this and that, then plunged further into the depths of the vast market, past a shop hung with filmy, sparkly belly dancers' outfits, and another piled high with ornate tiles and gleaming brass plates. To Ceri, it was a kind of wonderland. The smells, the sounds, the bustle, the exotic goods.

"Would you like to see some old Turkish carpets? Come, come... Drink some Turkish tea and I will explain."

The wiry middle-aged man with the thick black moustache smiled at them both and there was something about his dancing eyes and the animation in his face that made Ceri warm to him.

She looked at Paul. "Shall we?" she said. "I'd quite like to see some carpets. I can't afford to buy any, mind," she warned the salesman.

"That's OK," he said. "I like to talk about my carpets. I don't care if you don't buy. Just listen."

There was a dusty, friendly smell inside the shop that was somehow both romantic and nostalgic. It made Ceri think of old, crumbly, red rose petals from Valentine's Days of long ago.

The man told them about various carpets and showed them where they came from on a big map of Turkey. But time and again Ceri's eyes were drawn to a small carpet hanging on the wall. Its deep crimson was like those old red Valentine roses she had thought of. Its several shades of blue were the blues of sea and sky and misty hills and it had little yellow and green patterns which looked like flowers and birds.

"Could you tell us about that one?" Ceri said, pointing to it. "It's really beautiful."

"Ah!" the carpet man said. "That one is very special."

He took it down from the wall and laid it on top of the pile of carpets he had already shown them.

"Bride carpets usually come in twos, but I have only ever seen one like this one," he said.

"Bride? What do you mean?" Paul asked.

"This is what you call a dowry piece. We have a tradition that when a village girl is engaged to be married, she must make two carpets before her marriage, one for the house where she will live with her husband, and one for his parents. She makes them with love, and she weaves signs and symbols into them, wishing for happiness in her marriage. Sometimes she will weave her own initials into them, too. Come..."

He beckoned to Ceri. "Sit here, please, on the carpet."

Looking puzzled, Ceri did as she was bidden.

"Close your eyes, please," the man said. "Now make a wish, for you and your boyfriend. If you wish for happiness in love while sitting on this carpet, it will come true."

How embarrassing, thought Ceri. Paul wasn't her boyfriend. They had only just met. This might frighten him off altogether. She mustn't make any love wishes at all...

But she did, of course. She couldn't resist. The words just popped into her head. *Oh, please let this be a very special relationship. Let Paul love me passionately! Let it last for...* She was going to wish for *for ever*, but it seemed too soon to be wishing that, so she settled for *ages and ages*.

After they left the shop, Ceri looked for her mother's present and settled for a sweatshirt in her mother's favourite shade of blue, with a Turkish tile design on the front. The bazaar closed early in the winter and shoppers were already streaming towards the various exits. It was just after six.

"You're very quiet. Are you all right?" she asked Paul as they left the bazaar.

"Yes," he replied, lapsing into silence again.

Ceri got the distinct impression that something was wrong and a nasty, cold, niggly feeling started up inside her. If only they hadn't gone into the carpet shop. If only she hadn't gone along with that stupid "love wish" business!

They were almost at the hotel now and still Paul hadn't suggested any plans for that evening. She prayed her dad wouldn't insist on her spending the last night with him. Paul had to ask her out again, he just *had* to! He couldn't just say goodbye and walk out of her life...

Her father greeted them in high spirits. "Have a good afternoon, you two?" he enquired.

"Yes, great." Ceri was aware that she didn't sound very convincing. She stared at Paul, panic in her eyes and in her heart.

Then at last he spoke. "About tonight... Do you mind if I take Ceri out again, Mr Williams? Or have you made other arrangements?"

Ceri could feel her heartbeat thundering in her ears. *Go on, Dad*, she thought with all her mental strength, *say you'll let me go out with Paul. Please, please, I'll die if you don't!*

To her extreme relief, her father agreed.

Paul arranged to pick her up at eight, which gave Ceri time to shower and wash and dry her hair. She put on the white angora sweater which her grandmother had given her for Christmas, and brushed her long hair till it gleamed.

When Paul called for her, his mood seemed to have improved, much to Ceri's relief.

Perhaps he hadn't been feeling well, she thought. They ate spicy Turkish pizza in a tiny, dazzlingly clean *lokanta*, then went to a dance-bar at the top of a tall building with a fabulous view over the minarets of the Blue Mosque. It was the first time she and Paul had danced together. After a couple of fast records, the DJ put on a slow number and Paul put an arm round Ceri and pulled her towards him.

She leaned against him dreamily, her mind drifting back to the carpet and her wishes. His right hand was round her waist and his left hand stroked the locks of silky hair that coiled down the back of her fluffy jumper.

"So soft…" he murmured.

She didn't know whether he meant her hair or her sweater, and brushed the side of her face against his. In return, he nuzzled his nose and lips against her temple and gently nibbled her ear, sending shivers right through her. Then, very slowly, his lips glided over her cheek, found her mouth and settled there in a kiss that went on long after the record finished.

They came back just after one, Paul clasping her close to him as they walked slowly down the steep hill, staggering around pot-holes and broken kerbstones as if they were a pair of drunks. And though she had stuck to Coke all night, Ceri felt as though she *was* drunk – drunk on love and happiness.

Paul halted by a tree, some yards from the hotel door. "So – you go home tomorrow," he said.

Ceri held her breath, her heart pounding. *Here it comes*, she thought. *Any second now, I'll know whether it's just been a holiday romance, or whether he wants to see me again.*

"Manchester isn't that far from North Wales, is it?" he said.

"No, it's not," Ceri replied. Her hands were clenched in anxiety, her fingernails digging into her palms.

"So we could see each other again, if you'd like to..."

"Of course I'd like to." Ceri whispered the words. Something wasn't right – something in his voice, his expression. Something was ticking away like a time-bomb between them.

Then the bomb exploded.

"There's something I've got to tell you," he said. "It was on my mind all afternoon. I...

I haven't been entirely straight with you, Ceri. The fact is, I've got a girlfriend in Manchester. She—"

Ceri closed her ears. She didn't want to know. She could hear the frantic pounding of her heart; feel the hot, hurt tears springing into her eyes. How *could* he? Fancy leading her on like this, telling her how keen he was on her, getting her to fall in love with him, and all the while he had a girlfriend back home! He was a rat, a beast, she hated him!

She made to tear away from him and run into the hotel, but Paul caught her arm and pulled her back.

"Ceri... Ceri, I *know* you're upset but give me a chance to explain," he begged. "It's not like it seems."

"Oh *no*?" she responded bitterly.

"I can't blame you for being angry with me, but please listen. Tracey and I have been going out since last March but it's not working. We both know it, we've talked about it often enough, but as neither of us had met anyone else, we sort of let it wander on. As soon as I get back from Istanbul, I'm going to tell her about you and say I want out. I'm asking you to trust me,

Ceri. Will you do that?"

His grip on her arm was so tight it was hurting. But the pleading look in his eyes was hurting her more. "I'm asking you to wait for me, Ceri. I want you to know that I've fallen for you really heavily. Please believe me. If you feel the same way for me, then I'll finish with Tracey as soon as I get back. If you don't, then tell me now. Do you want to go out with me, or don't you?"

Ceri's face was a mask of unhappiness. "I... I don't know *what* I want," she faltered. "I... I don't just want you to finish with your steady girlfriend and hurt her, because of me. You've only just met me. It doesn't seem fair. But on the other hand, I really do want to go on seeing you. Oh, *Paul*..." Her voice cracked in agony.

"Tracey and I aren't in love with each other, it's a brother and sister kind of relationship. Oh, what's the use? How can I expect you to believe me?" He let go her wrist and dropped both hands by his sides in a gesture of total defeat.

Then he sighed again. "Don't make your mind up now," he said. "Think about it and let me know tomorrow. If you decide that, in spite of everything, you *do* want to go out with me, meet me outside that carpet shop in the bazaar at midday. OK?"

"OK." Ceri could scarcely force the word past her choking misery. He walked off and she stared after him for a moment, then pushed her way blindly into the hotel and pressed the lift button with a trembling finger, her vision blurred by tears.

When she got into her room, she flung herself on to her bed and cried.

"I can't see him, I mustn't, it wouldn't be fair," she moaned into her pillow. "Oh, why does he have to have a girlfriend? Why didn't he tell me at the start? Oh, Paul, Paul!"

She broke into a fresh storm of sobs. When they had finally subsided into dry, heaving gasps, she stumbled upright and staggered into the bathroom to splash her face and her hot, aching eyes with cold water. She looked at her dripping features in the mirror, staring blankly as if looking at a stranger.

"I love him," she spoke out loud. "I love you, Paul. I want to see you again... I've *got* to!" Why shouldn't she trust him and believe his story? She wondered what she would have done in his position, stuck in a draggy relationship that wasn't working any more, then suddenly meeting someone new whom you were really attracted to. Would she have told him right away that she already had a boyfriend at home? Of course not! That would have put him right off.

I'd have done just what Paul did, she decided. *I'd have waited until I was sure of my feelings for the new person – and their feelings for me – and then, only then, would I have told them about the situation.*

This realization made her spirits soar. Paul hadn't acted in an underhand manner. He was OK, after all. Moments later, she sank back into gloom. *If I did go out with him*, she thought, *how would I know what he was getting up to when he went back to Manchester? It would be quite easy for him to two-time me. I wouldn't know if he'd given up his other girlfriend or not...*

Ceri felt as if she were on a see-saw. On the up-swing she was believing and trusting Paul and turning up at the carpet shop to hurl herself into his arms and into a brand new relationship, while on the down-swing he was a deceitful, two-timing rat she never wanted to see again. After all, if he could be unfaithful to his Manchester girlfriend, wasn't he also perfectly capable of being unfaithful to her?

Oh, it was an impossible decision to make. It was a perfect case of heart and head colliding. "You love him, you must trust him," said her heart. "You can't trust him, you must give him up," said her head.

"I don't want any breakfast!" she shouted when her father tapped on her door next morning.

"Well, I've got to have mine now because I've got my final meeting at ten. I'll order a taxi for four o'clock. I'll be back here by three. You'd better be packed," her father said. "And remember, you mustn't go out on your own."

Ceri got up and showered, but the refreshing pounding of the water left her feeling no better. Sick in heart and spirit, she stared sadly through the window at the foggy blobs of ships on the hazy Bosphorus. She remembered the wish she'd made while sitting on the rug the previous day. How could she have been so stupid as to believe what that carpet man said? How many other people had been conned into doing the same thing? He probably had hundreds of those rugs in the back of the shop, and made a fortune out of them, she thought cynically. Magic carpet, indeed! Fat lot of good it was at making *her* dreams come true.

She sat down defeatedly on a bedside chair and looked at her watch. Almost eleven-twenty. In forty minutes' time Paul would be waiting for her outside the carpet shop, anxious to hear her decision. Her brain felt like a washing machine on fast spin. She got up, went over to the mini-bar and took out a cold Coke. Swigging it cleared her head. Paul's face appeared in close-up in her mind's eye. She felt once again the touch of his lips, heard his voice saying, "Wait for me ... trust me... I've fallen for you really heavily."

"I love you, Paul, I really do," she murmured. And suddenly she knew what she had to do. She pulled on her boots, threw on her coat, stuffed her gloves into her pocket and slammed out of her room. Within minutes, regardless of her father's orders, she was racing up the hill towards the bazaar.

Which street was it? Ceri gazed frantically

this way and that. They all looked the same. Everywhere she looked there were jewellery shops, ceramic shops, T-shirt shops. Ah, there was a carpet shop. It had to be down there...

Ten past twelve. He'd be there. It didn't matter that she didn't know the name of the shop, she was bound to spot him standing waiting outside it.

A quarter past... Ceri was panting as she barged through crowds of tourists and elbowed people aside in her haste to find the shop. *It has to be down this street... No, no sign of it. Let's try this one. Oh Paul, where are you?*

By quarter to one, she had given up. In fact, she realized she had been going round in circles when she passed the coffee bar on the corner for the fourth time. She collapsed into a cold metal chair and buried her face in her gloved hands. A waiter started hassling her to order something and she abruptly got up and ran away, finding an exit almost by instinct. As she came out from under the covered bazaar, a billow of driving sleet lashed her in the face and she staggered, pulling her scarf up around her mouth.

Head down, she braced herself against the

icy, buffeting wind, feeling glad of its cutting coldness as it matched the bleak chill inside her. She'd blown it, she really, truly had. Paul would think she had rejected him and he would already be trying to forget her. She would never, ever see him again. Her face was so numb with cold that she could no longer feel the tears pouring down it.

"Here, pretty lady. Perfumes!" A man was at her side, walking too close, nudging her, pushing a box of perfumes at her. He touched her arm and leered, showing teeth that were cracked and brown.

"Go away!" Ceri screamed. She broke into a run, tearing up the narrow street. More men called out to her, made hissing noises at her. She had never felt more terrified in her life.

She was at the main road now. The tram-lines were in front of her and tears and sleet were blinding her eyes.

"You are lost? Can I help you?" The voice was oily and came from a gaunt, sinister looking man in a heavy grey overcoat.

Ceri made a stumbling dash across the road. Something hooted at her and a lorry swished by, sending a wave of dirty water up the backs of her legs. She was sobbing out loud now, not caring who heard as she cut down the street opposite, shouldering people aside in her panic. She headed downhill, knowing that somewhere she would find a road that joined the one her hotel was in. Her father had been right – being a lone female on the streets of Istanbul was an utterly terrifying experience.

Oh Paul, Paul... she thought longingly. *Where are you?* If only he would appear like magic to guide both her and her emotions back to safety. But Paul was gone ... she would never see him again and her hot tears mingled with the icy rain and her feet slowed to a shuffle as the weakness of fear and desolation invaded her from the inside out.

And then she saw it – the familiar flagpoles and doorway of the Grand Yavus. Like a drowning person up for their last gasp of life-giving air, she pushed open the doors and stumbled into the foyer, drenched to the bone. Inside, there was no sign of Paul. When she asked for her key, she prayed to be handed a note, but there was nothing. He was gone – truly gone.

Once in her room, she packed like an

automaton, not bothering to fold anything, just chucking her things in, until her body was so racked with great, shuddering sobs that she curled up into a tight ball on her bed and cried as if she would never stop.

She told her father that she was starting a cold. It was the only way to explain her red eyes, pale face and snuffling nose. They travelled to the airport in silence and once there, Mr Williams went to find a trolley for their bags, leaving Ceri standing alone, their luggage in a heap at her feet.

Suddenly, a package wrapped in brown paper appeared from nowhere and landed on top of the bags.

"Think you can carry another one?" enquired a voice.

"Paul! I don't believe it! How did you...? What...?"

Her words were stopped by his mouth crushing on to hers. She tried to push him away. "Dad'll be back in second," she said breathlessly.

"All the more reason to kiss you now," Paul said huskily.

When the long, long kiss came to an end, Ceri said, "I couldn't find the shop. I got lost. I was really upset. I was sure you'd think I'd decided not to see you again."

"I wouldn't have blamed you in the slightest," Paul said, with a sad little smile and a shrug. "But I just had to come and try and find you here, just to be sure. I wanted one last chance to persuade you that I was telling you the truth about me and Tracey. Please, Ceri, say you believe me..."

The expression on his face left her in no doubt that his story was true. Even a professional actor would have been hard pushed to manufacture quite such an anguished, pleading expression. "Yes, I believe you, Paul," she whispered.

"Oh, Ceri..." He swept her into his arms again and this time she didn't try to push him away, simply surrendered her lips to his passionate kiss.

"You'd better write down your phone number," Paul said when, reluctantly, they broke apart.

Ceri took her diary out of her bag, tore out a page and scribbled down the number.

"Don't be surprised if you get a call tonight," he said. "By the way, aren't you going to open your present?"

"Present? I didn't know it was something

for me," she said.

She picked it up and, unable to unfasten the knot in the string, she tore the paper in one corner. Shades of deep crimson and blue revealed themselves. Woven with love, she thought. Full of hopes and dreams — love spells that were already starting to come true.

Just as she was hugging Paul and thanking him, the edge of an airport trolley nudged the heap of baggage.

"Come on, you two, say your goodbyes. We don't want to miss the plane," said Ceri's dad.

"It doesn't matter about me," said Ceri. "I've got a magic carpet to fly home on."

An Unhappy Christmas and a Happy New Year

Bette Paul

When Caitlin saw the yellow envelope her heart sank. She stood quite still, and stared at the wire box on the back of the door.

"No post?" asked Bella, friend and flat-mate. She reached in front of Caitlin, flicked up the box lid and scooped out the contents. "Mmmm – number three – they get junk mail, would you believe? Number five – air letter – from his mother, I'll bet! Aha – here we have it – number seven – our very own abode!" She flicked through the remaining envelopes. "And here's one mighty missive for you, darlin'!" Bella held out the yellow envelope.

"Thanks," said Caitlin, and she stuffed the letter in her duffel-coat pocket without even looking at it.

Her lack of enthusiasm was not lost on Bella.

"Hey – surely that was from Himself?"

She scrutinized her friend's face. "Don't I remember a time when the very sight of a yellow envelope would bring a blush to that delicate cheek, a tearful shine to those china-blue eyes and a dance into your every step?"

"Do shut up, Bella," said Caitlin, mildly. Bella could be very irritating at times. "I'm in a hurry, that's all – must dash – see you later."

"Lunch in the Black Hole – and you can tell all."

"There's nothing to tell and I can't afford lunch." Caitlin made a dash for the door. "See you this evening – 'bye!"

And before she slammed the door she heard Bella's scornful comment.

"Nothing to tell – I'll bet!"

But it was true, Caitlin reflected as she pulled up her hood and ducked her way through the icy rain. There really was nothing to tell. Perhaps that was the trouble: if only she was having a mad affair with someone else – or better still, if Gavin was – that would sort things out. For a few seconds her heart lifted. Maybe he was? Maybe this was a "dear Jane" letter, telling her how he'd met this wonderful girl back home...

But she knew it would be the same kind of letter he'd been writing every week since she'd come to college: heart-warming and guilt-inducing. Though she had nothing to feel guilty about, she reflected, not even a casual date with any one else. And why? as Bella was for ever asking. Because of Gavin, sweet and tender, loving and caring – and waiting for her at home. Caitlin groaned and huddled deep into her duffel and staggered across the wind-swept campus to her first lecture of the day.

At lunchtime, in order to avoid the "Black Hole" crowd congregating in the basement refectory, she took herself off to the library, seated herself in a dim corner and opened Gavin's letter. For a moment she stared at it as if it was in a foreign language, unheeding. Then, with a great sigh, she bent her head and started, reluctantly, to read.

Dear, darling love – my Caitlin, he addressed her, as always.

Only two days and you'll be here where you belong – in my arms. Five weeks we've been apart and it's felt like five years. Well, at least we'll have a whole month together now – and Christmas too! We've been invited to four parties, a couple of discos and three gigs, not to mention the family gatherings. But it's the evenings at home alone together I'm looking forward to.

I can just hear you saying "But I've got work to do!" Well, so have I. Dad's idea of a Christmas holiday is three hours for a turkey dinner then back to the office! Still, I think you'll charm him into letting me have a few days off. God knows he owes me plenty – I've never missed a day since I left school.

But then, I don't mind. Life without you is so boring I have nothing else to do but work. And play rugger, of course – we had a great game against St Ermyn's last weekend...

Caitlin's eyes glazed over. One of the many hazards of being Welsh was that you were supposed to be madly musical or mad on rugby – or, preferably, both. She was neither. Skipping the sporting news, she glanced down to the end of the letter:

... so that'll mean the Rugby Club Ball will be extra special this year – we're on our way to winning the championship at last. And I mean to make it extra-special for us, my darling – I've got a big surprise for you. If I write any more I won't be able to stop myself telling you so I'd better finish.

Your lonely, loving – and, by now, longing, Gavin.

There followed rows and rows of kisses to fill up the page. Though, typically, Gavin had obviously counted them.

PS That's one a day for all the days we've missed plus one for each day of the holidays. Keep us busy many a day, they will – and maybe the occasional night, who knows?

She folded the letter up very carefully and slipped it back in its envelope. She gazed around the library, blankly, tears in her eyes. What was she going to do about Gavin? Well, that was quite simple – she had to finish with him, she knew that. But how? And when? She wouldn't be home until the day before the Rugby Club dance – the event of the year as far as Gavin was concerned. She couldn't jilt him then. And afterwards there'd be Christmas Eve at her house, Christmas Dinner at his, Boxing Day at his sister's, those four parties, the gigs, the school reunion in the New Year. It would go on and on and on... Gavin and Caitlin, a couple, a pair, an item – everybody knew that, they'd been going around together since year nine.

Caitlin shoved the letter back into the

pocket of her jeans with shaking hands. Shaking hands? Bella would shake her if she saw her in this state. Thinking about Bella, Caitlin managed a wobbly smile. It was all right for her – she juggled fellas and dates like other girls juggled course-work and exams. And she never, not ever, felt any qualms, any pangs of guilt, at saying, clearly and distinctly – "No." And in half-a-dozen languages too.

But then, Bella had been brought up in Europe, not in a tight-knit Welsh community. She'd lived amongst the economists, politicians, scientists of the EC, gone to school with their children – the *jeunesse d'orée* of Europe. Back home, Caitlin was the golden one, regarded with envy and admiration because she'd caught the most eligible bachelor in the district. And Gavin wasn't just eligible, he was the kindest, most generous, thoughtful, loving … the *nicest*…

Caitlin choked back the tears. What was she going to do about Gavin?

"It's simple – don't go!" Bella declared.

"Don't go where?" Caitlin couldn't believe what she was hearing. It was late that night when she'd finally cracked, confessed all, begged Bella for advice and now she was drained. "What do you mean?" she asked.

"Home – don't go home."

There was silence. Caitlin stared at Bella as if she'd just suggested something indecent.

"I can't do that," she whispered.

"Yes you can," Bella assured her. "Ring them up and tell them you've got a great invitation to the flesh-pots of Brussels." She grinned. "On second thoughts, leave the flesh-pots out," she said. "I forgot about your Presbyterian susceptibilities."

"But your parents haven't invited me," Caitlin objected.

"I'm inviting you now."

"I can't just turn up at your family Christmas," Caitlin objected.

"Why not – my brother will be bringing some giggling bimbo or other, my sister always has a chinless wonder in tow – why shouldn't I bring a friend home?"

For a moment Caitlin was tempted. Not so much by the idea of a holiday in Brussels – that was hardly her idea of abroad – but by the thought of getting away from family pressures – and from Gavin.

"Thanks," she said, eventually. "But no, thanks."

"You going to do the honourable thing?" asked Bella.

"You mean marry him?" asked Caitlin, horrified.

Bella burst into laughter.

"There you are, you see," she pointed out. "The very thought of marrying the guy frightens you." She turned serious for a moment. "Look, Caitlin, love, you're going to have to get this thing straightened out before next term. It's really getting to you – soon it'll be affecting your work as well as your social life, and we have exams next term."

"I know," Caitlin sighed. "The trouble is, once I get home I'm part of Gavin's life once again and I can't break loose."

Bella looked thoughtful.

"Look – it's like giving up any other habit. Because that's all he is – a habit. You've been going around together since your early teens – been everywhere together for four years now – you're a Gavin addict. You've just got to learn to give him up."

Caitlin smiled briefly. "If that's your diagnosis," she asked, "what's the prescription for a cure?"

Bella looked at her seriously. "I can't cure you," she said. "But I can help you convalesce…"

Gavin Howarth stood at the barrier watching the train pull in. He had no need to strain, being several inches taller than anyone else in the waiting crowd, and yet, as the air-brakes sighed and doors clattered open, he couldn't stop himself peering forward eagerly. Yes – there she was! He raised a hand in greeting but she didn't see him. Gavin smiled and shook his head slightly – she probably hadn't put her lenses in and couldn't see at that distance.

He could. He watched her every step as she trotted along the platform towards him, neat and nimble, strong and steady, bags swinging in both hands – his Catey! Smiling broadly, he stepped back and opened out his arms.

"Catey!" he bellowed. Oblivious of the startled looks around him he swept her up into his arms. "Welcome home, my lovely!" he murmured.

She stood stiffly, clutching her bags, submitting to his embrace rather than responding, screwing up her face and closing her eyes. Was that an expression of ecstasy? he wondered.

"Oh Catey!" he breathed in her ear. "It's been such a long time."

"Five weeks, actually." Caitlin laughed nervously and extricated herself. "I was home for half-term weekend, remember?"

"Was it only five weeks ago?" He took her bags. "Feels more like five years, doesn't it?"

And he looked down at her slightly quizzically, waiting for her to agree. But she just gave him one of her quick smiles and stepped briskly out alongside him.

"You've got the car?" she asked.

"Of course." Gavin grinned down at her. "One of the perks of working in the family business. And there's going to be a few developments at Howarth and Sons," he added, deliberately casual. Ah – that got her interested, he noted, as she turned to look up at him in surprise. "Tell you more later," he said. She'd have to be satisfied with that.

"Gavin meet you at the station?" enquired her Nain – her very Welsh grandmother. "There's nice!"

"Nice" was what everyone said about her

going out with Gavin. Right from the start her family had been impressed, her friends frankly incredulous: Gavin Howarth was the catch of the valley – intelligent, athletic, beautiful – and rich! Thanks to Euromoney, government investment and Mrs Howarth's fierce ambition, Howarth and Sons had been transformed from a local haulage contractor to the biggest trucking business in the west.

Even so, Gavin Howarth went to the local schools, joined the local rugby club, charmed the local girls – popular, modest and thoroughly "nice". And one of the few local boys to have a secure future. What more could any girl ask? Caitlin often asked herself. Nothing – that was what her family and friends so obviously thought.

Nain was looking closely at her now. "There's a nice boy Gavin, now," she observed. "Never changed, d'you see."

"Yes, Nain," Caitlin sighed. "He's never changed."

"Nor have you," said her mother, briskly. "You'll need to get your hair done for tomorrow night – I'll give Sandra a ring."

Sandra ran the salon at the end of the road, where the local ladies had their perms, their blow-dries and their grey hairs tinted. Caitlin had a sudden vision of herself after Sandra's dramatic treatment: henna-red highlights with a mass of glossy gelled curls.

"It'll be all right when I've washed it," she said, mildly.

Her mother frowned. "You'll need more than a pony-tail and a plastic bobble for the Rugby Club dance with Gavin Howarth," she said.

Caitlin knew what she was thinking: a bit of investment now would pay for itself and more in later years...

"I'll wash it and wear it down," she said, firmly.

"And what are you going to wear?" her mother went on. "We'll go shopping for a dress in the morning – your Christmas present, from Dad and Nain and me."

"Oh, Mum – you mustn't." Money was very tight just then, with her dad on his third redundancy. "I got just the thing from the charity shop in Hampstead."

"Charity shop?" Her mother was appalled.

"Yes, but the Hampstead shop isn't like our Oxfam, you know. Designer labels, cruise-wear worn once only, wedding dresses worth a thousand..."

She could have bitten her tongue out. Her mother brightened visibly at the mention of weddings.

"Well, there's nice, I'm sure," she tut-tutted. "Fancy buying a second-hand dress for a bride!"

"Better than no dress at all, eh, Caitlin?" Nain smiled naughtily. "Wore my chapel coat, I did, and Glyn in his uniform..." Her eyes grew misty.

It was high time to change the subject. Caitlin stood up.

"Well, I got a hardly-ever-worn Laura Ashley for ten pounds," she said. "Want to come upstairs and see it?"

Rugby Club dances were always held on Fridays, leaving Saturday morning for recovery, the afternoon for play, followed by a night out with the lads. A pity in a way, Gavin thought, recklessly splashing after-shave around his face. Saturday night would be neater – finish up the week and start afresh next day. Of course his chapel-going days were over now, but even so, Sunday still had a special feel in Wales. His dad could remember the days when Sunday was "dry" and he had to bike twenty miles to the border to get a drink. Of course that was all changed now and this Sunday he'd be taking Caitlin along to The Dragon for pre-Christmas lunch with his parents. Pre-Christmas and post-proposal, with any luck.

Gavin smiled at his reflection in the mirror. Not too bad considering ten years play: nose beyond repair – they said they'd do it when he gave up rugby – several teeth crowned – and re-crowned – and an interesting scar across one cheek. Made him more attractive, the girls said – though not Caitlin. She said it didn't matter either way – it wasn't his nose or his teeth she loved, it was himself.

And it was himself, he was sure of that. The other girls had been fun, some had been very nearly serious, but there'd never been anybody like Caitlin Edwards – serious and honest and true. When she said she loved him for himself he knew she meant just that, not for his money or his father's business – or even for his beauty! He grinned to himself as he buttoned up the creamy silk shirt which was going to cause some comment from his dad.

Like others of his generation – retired from the field but still ardently supporting the club – his father would turn out tonight in dinner jacket and black tie. But the younger players favoured the casual, trendy look of jersey shirt, draped jacket and black chinos.

Of course Gavin did possess the full evening kit – had to, with his job and family – but he knew Caitlin didn't and he wanted to fit in with her, to show everyone they belonged together – especially tonight.

He pulled on his best pair of slacks – dark blue against the cream of the shirt, flicked his well-cut hair down and reached for his jacket – a very expensive Italian job, which sat snugly on his broad shoulders and draped comfortingly around his hefty thighs. Then he picked up his wallet, credit cards, keys to his mother's car – Dad was very strict about company car use – and finally, a small, square box, neatly wrapped in gold paper and tied with metallic ribbon. Pity about that – it made a bulge in the jacket pocket.

"Still," he told himself. "It won't be there for long."

* * *

The Laura Ashley was just right, as she'd known it would be. Bella had teased her about it. "Seventies retro?" she'd asked when Caitlin had picked it out. But there was nothing retro about the Rugby Club dance; it was ageless: sun ray pleated georgette shirts swirled past skin-tight Lycra minis and power-shouldered sequined tops. The only fashion rule was to wear something new, something never seen before. Difficult that, for those who lived in Pendine, easier for Caitlin, having missed the last two Rugby Club dances. Nevertheless, she was well aware of the speculative stares as she entered the bar on Gavin's arm.

"Gavin – and here she is – Caitlin – my, how you've changed!" This was Sandy Beresford, captain of the Rugby Club.

Caitlin blushed. She knew he was not referring to her character but to the all-covering dark green dress. When she'd lived at home, she'd followed the trend – miniskirts, opalescent tights, lycra tops. This dress had a fitted bodice with a dropped waistline; the flowing skirt fell just above her neat ankles. It was the epitome of modesty – until your eye was drawn to the deeply scooped neckline.

"All right for some!" was Bella's summing-up. "You've got just the right figure." And she'd given her a pair of dangly jet earrings to go with the dress.

Caitlin's mother had winced at the neckline and offered to lend her pearls – at present tucked into Caitlin's bag in the cloakroom.

Nain had said, "There's nice, lovely!" and handed over a beautiful dark red Paisley shawl. "Don't want you catching cold, now, do we?" she'd smiled.

The other girls greeted Caitlin coolly, surprised by her new look. They were all into big hair, long legs, tight-and-shiny frocks and here was Caitlin Edwards, supposedly from the world centre of fashion, looking like a governess in a period film. She'd brushed her dark hair into smooth wings either side of her face, her fringe low on her brow, and used no make-up at all, save a little lip-gloss.

Gavin drew her into the crowd, tucking her hand into his.

"The usual?" he asked her.

And, to save trouble, she nodded, though she could have downed a mug of Nain's extra-strong tea with two sugars rather than white wine just then.

"Glad to see you back, girl," said Sandy as he watched Gavin move over to the bar. "Been on hot bricks all week, he has."

Caitlin caught an overtone of disapproval, as if that were her fault, and she wasn't sure what she was supposed to say to everyone listening. Luckily the band struck up just then and the attention turned away from her.

The first hour or two was live music from a six-piece band made up of local amateurs, playing anything from a quick-step through Latin-American to a bit of mild jiving. After the buffet supper there'd be a disco, and the older members would gradually fade out, leaving the youngsters to take over both dancefloor and bar.

"Dance?" Gavin asked her, when he returned.

And again, to save trouble, she nodded.

She regretted it though. She'd quite forgotten how well he danced. How she fitted snug up to his chest when he held her close. How they sensed each other's every move so that they danced without straining, echoing the rhythms of the music, a turn here, a twist there. And they never spoke. It wouldn't have been easy anyway, with Gavin towering above her, but they never had, right from the start at their first school disco – they'd always concentrated on each other, dancing silently and seriously.

Of course she danced with other people too; that was allowed – encouraged – in their circles. Even the one or two engaged couples split and circulated amongst their friends, just to socialize, though they made it clear they weren't really available. She caught Gavin's eye as he stepped around the floor with Sandy's fiancée, a tall red-head, who rested her hand on his shoulder to display a sparkling solitaire on her left hand. Gavin grimaced slightly and winked. Caitlin smiled, – then wished she hadn't, because it seemed to draw them together into some kind of conspiracy, and that was the last thing she wanted.

She ate hardly any supper, but then, few of the girls did. Rugby Club buffets consisted of giant pasties and sausage rolls like bats, hundreds of sandwiches – sliced white, of course – stuffed with local ham, and sharp, strong cheese, all this "garnished" with bowls of hard-boiled eggs and crisps of various flavours. The only concession to anyone mad enough to like vegetables came in the form of huge brown pickled onions and great clumps of celery stuck in beer-mugs at intervals along the table.

"There's grand, isn't it?" commented the president's wife, tucking her brocade evening bag firmly into her armpit and piling up her plate.

The boys piled theirs up several times, refilled their pints several more times, the talk got louder, the laughter lewder and Caitlin wondered how she'd last until after midnight, which would be the earliest Gavin would want to move.

"You all right, Caitlin?" Gavin leaned over and spoke into her ear. "Only you look a bit pale, like."

For a moment she was tempted to take the easy way out. She had only to plead feeling unwell for him to fetch the car round and run her home. After all, he'd done that often enough when she went through that awful patch of migraine before A-levels. If she left now he could be back in time for the disco. But he wouldn't, she knew that. He'd drop her off, see her settled in and go home alone, disappointed for her rather than for himself.

There's kind, now, isn't it? she mocked herself in the local lingo. No, what she had to do was bad enough without lying to Gavin.

"I'm fine," she lied. "It's just a bit noisy…"

"I know somewhere where it's very quiet," he whispered into her ear. "Come on!" He stood up and pulled her after him.

"Where're you two going?" asked Sandy Beresford, loudly.

Gavin waved him away and gave a broad wink.

"Oooohhhh!" chorused the gang, knowingly. And – "Bit early for that, boy, isn't it?" added Sandy. Gavin pulled a face and made a rude gesture as he ushered Caitlin out.

Of course she knew where they were going: there were several small lounges in the club house, all comfortably furnished with big sofas and deep armchairs, in which the committee members could relax, after a hard evening's moaning about league points, tables and missed tries.

But on an evening like this it was their sons and daughters who drifted into the lounges to relax. Later on there wouldn't be a seat to be had – not even a spare lap!

But now, as Gavin led Caitlin across the deep-pile carpet, there was only the shape of the heavy furniture outlined by the orange beam from the security light outside. It was dim and silent and still, and Caitlin's heart sank as she recognized that the moment of truth had arrived.

"Gavin..." she began.

"Shhh." He put his finger to her lips. "Come and sit down."

He led her to one of the big sofas, sat himself in a corner and pulled her after him.

And then he kissed her.

It was like the first sip of a pint after a match, he decided. The first cup of tea in the morning. Like the first time they'd ever kissed – though that must be years ago now. He lifted his head briefly and breathed deeply, the better to savour the moment.

"Ahhhh, Caitlin," he muttered. And bent for seconds.

No need to rush now, no need to worry, he told himself. She was here at last, with him, for him, for ever. No need to pretend to be sociable now, he had her to himself. The rest of Christmas there would be friends and family all over them, but for the moment it was just the two of them.

"Gavin?" she gasped.

"Shhhhh," he said, placing his lips on hers.

No point in resisting yet, she thought. It would turn into an undignified struggle and he might take it the wrong way. What wrong way? Was there ever going to be a right one? Trembling now, she lifted her face to his.

"Gavin?" she pleaded. "We have to..."

But he hadn't heard – or didn't want to. Obviously taking her trembling as acquiescence he pressed her close to him and kissed her again. And to her dismay, Caitlin found herself responding, not rejecting.

"Gavin," she groaned, half to herself. This was not how it was meant to be. She should be telling him, quietly, assertively, of her needs – not responding to his! But he was so hugely attractive, so physical, so ... well ... sexy.

"Relax, it's all right, my darling," he breathed.

But it wasn't. Caitlin breathed deeply, shaking with the sheer effort of trying to keep her head when all around...

What was he doing? She suddenly felt his arm loosen, his hand scrabble along her back into his jacket pocket. What was he looking for?

"Gavin!" she suddenly pulled away in alarm. Oh God, she'd played it all wrong. Now it was going to turn into an undignified struggle – the worst kind of struggle! Caitlin cursed her own clumsiness. She should never have allowed him to bring her into the lounge – everyone knew that was the prelude to some very heavy petting...

Holding her tightly with one strong hand behind her back, Gavin fumbled in his pocket with the other. Damn and blast the thing – it was caught in the lining!

"Sorry, Caitlin," he gasped. And then he groaned. "Sorry my love – if you could just ease up..."

There – he'd got it!

Just ease up? Caitlin took the opportunity to sit upright and fling herself into the farthest corner of the sofa.

"Gavin – we need to talk," she said, unsteadily.

"I know we do," he soothed. "Just wait a moment till I've got this sorted out..."

Caitlin wondered whether she ought to

flee there and then – out of the dimly-lit lounge, across the bright club room – and out into the night...

But how could she – in full public view? She couldn't let Gavin down like that, leave him to face all their friends. Not Gavin, nice, loyal, generous Gavin.

But Gavin was still talking. "I've been wanting to tell you since you got back. You've no idea how hard it's been, keeping it all to myself."

"What do you mean?" she asked, cautiously. For a moment hope flamed: maybe he was the one doing the jilting? Maybe the previous little scene was his final farewell? But she knew Gavin would never play things that way. Unlike her, Gavin had courage.

"Oh, Caitlin," he was saying now. "I know you've a long way to go to your degree, I know you'll say it's too soon. But why waste time when we're both so sure?"

She could see his eyes glinting in the light from the window, hear the confidence in his voice. He was so sure of her, she thought, with sudden irritation. And what the hell was he fiddling with over there? She could see something shiny, hear the metallic crinkle of paper... She shuddered. No, that settled it – she couldn't go through with all that and then tell him to push off. That wasn't the way.

"No, Gavin," she said, in a small clear voice. "I'm not sure at all – not even sure what you're talking about."

"No, of course not," he said, reaching for her hand, easily. "That's my fault – I haven't explained everything yet."

He went on talking – at length, about his father's plans for expansion, about the new depot close to the Channel Tunnel, within easy reach of London, about his going to work there – manage it eventually, maybe even move over the Channel – and then her language degree would come in useful, wouldn't it?

"So you see, my darling, it's all falling into place..." He moved over towards her. "Next year's going to be the biggest, brightest year of our lives – here!" He suddenly thrust the metallic package at her. "Go on, take it – an early Christmas present, if you like." He pressed it into her hand.

Caitlin shrank back into her corner, clutching the box. It was a box, she knew that now, by the shape of it. And she almost laughed aloud at her mistake – Bella would have enjoyed that! The sudden thought of Bella gave her confidence – and common sense.

"If this is what I think it is," she said, carefully, "I can't possibly accept it."

There, it was out. She felt suddenly stronger. She could even look across at him now.

For the first time he faltered.

"What do you mean?" he asked. "Look, don't worry about the cost – it was my gran's ring – not even very valuable. I want you to have it."

Caitlin shook her head.

"I couldn't possibly," she said.

"Why not? I mean, if it's not good enough for an engagement ring, you could have it as a memento – wear it on any old finger…" He was beginning to sound desperate.

Caitlin took a deep and shaky breath. "I'm flattered – honoured, that you should want to give your gran's ring to me," she said. "But it won't do, Gavin. Not this ring, not a diamond solitaire, not anything. Because we're not engaged."

"You mean I haven't proposed?" He clapped a hand to his head. "Oh God, I'm sorry, Caitlin – I mean I really did think – oh, I'm a stupid fool. Look – I mean – you will marry me, won't you?"

He reached out for her. She edged back.

"No," she said. Such a little word – why couldn't she have said it sooner – months ago?

"What?"

"No, I won't marry you," she said, softly.

"But why not? I mean we've been together all this time and..."

"All this time – that's the trouble, Gavin. We've been together too long, not given each other a chance to breathe, to grow, explore, experiment." She sighed. "We're like an old married couple already!" she burst out, then sat back, waiting for the tirade of protests.

But Gavin said nothing. He just sat there, almost without breathing. He felt as if he'd just been hit in the stomach; if he opened his mouth he'd vomit. Was this his Caitlin? he asked himself. The girl who'd wept for hours before he'd put her on the London train last September? The girl who'd phoned every night the first week or two in college? Didn't now, of course – but then, he'd assumed that was because she'd got settled in. He turned slowly, stiffly, to face her.

"So, you see, I want out," she was saying, in that cool, musical voice of hers. "I'm going to Brussels for New Year – I think I'd better go straight after the family Christmas, out of your way, save you any embarrassment…"

"Embarrassment?" He'd found his voice. "Is that all you think I'll be feeling?" He choked on his anguish. "Caitlin, I love you – I've loved you for years now, waited for you – happy to go on waiting for you to finish your degree. I'm not asking you to give it all up, not even asking you to be engaged, if you think that's a bit naff. All I'm asking is for us to go on loving each other." His voice cracked.

"But that's just what I can't do," she said, gently. "I've moved on, Gavin, away from all this." She gestured to the room and out to the club house beyond. "Away from the rugby and the parents and the family and friends – I want to be free of all that for a while – maybe for a long while, I don't know." She sighed. "I just know I want a bit of my youth back before it's too late. A bit of a different date every weekend and no strings attached. A bit of no man in my life at all, if that's how it turns out. A bit of peace." She sat back, exhausted. She could hear his breath rasping, uneven, sobbing.

"You mean you've met someone?"

Caitlin groaned. "You haven't been listening," she said. "There's nobody else, Gavin. Nobody as generous, as loving, as thoroughly nice as you are – in fact, nobody at all. I'm going to stay with Bella in Brussels, taste a little of European high life, practise my languages, then go back to college and get on with the rest of my course – the rest of my life. That's all." She leaned over and took his large hand in both of hers. "Sorry," she said.

Gavin felt as if he'd split in pieces. He shook his head and felt the tears spatter down his shirt. Would they stain his new jacket? he wondered, stupidly. He couldn't speak – there was nothing to say anyway. Without actually feeling as if he were crying, he knew the tears continued to stream down his face. His nose was running, his mouth dry...

"I'm so, so sorry," said Caitlin again, and this time he felt her tears on his hand, mingling with his. For some reason that gave him a sort of comfort. He clung on to her hand, falling, drowning.

"I didn't want this to happen," she was saying. "I wanted it all to stay like it was at school." She, too, was sobbing now. "But it won't, Gavin – we won't. We have to grow up, move on..."

They sat close, quite still, holding hands, as if they'd never let go, never move again. He heard a burst of laughter from the club room, then the tinkle of broken glass – things were getting lively in there, he thought, wearily, as if he were an old, old man.

Suddenly she thrust his hand away and stood up, pulling her shawl around her.

" 'Bye, Gavin," she muttered. "I'll get a taxi home."

"No – Catey – please..." He clung on to the skirt of her dress, burying his face in it, taking in her perfume in great gasps. "Please – I can't let you go like this!"

"Yes, you can – you have to!" she cried, tugging at her skirt. "Let me go, Gavin! Let me go!"

And they both knew she meant for ever.

He stood up beside her, unsteadily. "Not on your own, not like this," he said, quietly now. "Look, you don't want to face everybody now, do you?"

She shook her head, miserably. Trust Gavin to consider her feelings even when she was hurting him so much.

"We'll go out the back to the car park," he said quietly. "And I'll drive you straight home." She started to protest but he cut her short. "I'll be worried if I don't."

Outside, while Gavin unlocked the car, Caitlin stood for a moment, huddled in Nain's shawl, staring up at the sky where ragged clouds blew across the moon and spats of rain combined with the tears on her face.

"I'm so sorry, Gavin," she murmured, over and over. "So very sorry…" She mopped her wet face with the fringes of the shawl.

"Get in," he ordered, and as soon as she was settled he drove her home in a silence broken only by her occasional sobbing breath, his dismal sniff.

As he pulled in she opened her mouth to speak, though she had no idea what she could say, except "sorry" again and again. She needn't have worried: Gavin was his usual thoughtful self. He leapt out and came round to open her door. Caitlin clambered unsteadily out and stood before him.

"You're sure about this?" he asked.

She nodded dumbly, wishing only to escape up the garden path, into the house, up to her room...

He took her hand, looked at it for a moment, then kissed it, gently – politely, almost.

"Well then, goodbye, Catey," he murmured. Then suddenly he caught his breath in a sob and turned back to the car. As he pulled away, Caitlin could see the glimmer of tears on his face.

"Gavin!" she called – though it was only an agonized whisper, lost in the wind and the rain. Pulling the shawl over her head, she watched until the car disappeared down the hill. "Goodbye," she murmured – to Gavin, to the rosy future she'd just thrown away.

"Gavin bring you home last night, *cariad*?" Nain asked Caitlin, when she finally emerged from her room late next morning.

"Yes, Nain, he did," she said.

"There's nice now, isn't it?" said Nain. "There's a lovely boy he is." She smiled quizzically at Caitlin. "Be round tomorrow, I expect?"

Caitlin took a deep, deep breath. Well, she had to start somewhere.

"Well, actually, Nain, he won't," she said. And to her surprise her voice sounded firm and strong – and, well, almost happy.

Out in the Cold

Helen McCann

Emma pulled her collar up round her ears as she and Jassy ran across the college campus on their way to lunch. Stinging needles of rain were turning to sleet now and the sky was dark with huge black clouds. It looked as if there was even worse weather on the way. Everywhere, students were hurrying like ants from building to building, dashing to get in, out of the cold and wet. In front of them, the lights of the refectory gleamed their welcome.

Emma buried her nose deeper in the thick woolly scarf wound round her neck. Dave's scarf. The one he had taken off and given to her on that chill October day when he'd left for France. She could still smell the faintest trace of his aftershave. It brought the whole scene back to her.

They were standing in the draughty bus station with the sharp October wind whistling round them.

"The training course only lasts for one term," Dave said. "I'll be back at Christmas."

Emma tried to smile but her mouth wouldn't cooperate.

"All that way," she said. "You'll forget all about me."

Dave had looked at her then, his dark blue eyes troubled, his hair ruffled by the wind. Emma felt the breath catch in her throat. He was so good-looking it wasn't real.

"I'll never do that," he said seriously.

"What about all those French girls at the ski resort?" she said, trying to make a joke of it. "You know what they say about ski instructors."

"I'm not a ski instructor yet. Just training to be one," Dave said.

Emma looked up at him. She would have to get used to it. If Dave was going to become a professional sports instructor he was going to have girls falling over themselves at the sight of him.

"And I won't even notice the French girls," said Dave, bending to kiss her.

But they'll notice you, Emma thought as she clung to him. That was when he had given her his scarf. Lifting his head from the long, long kiss he took the scarf, still warm from his neck, and wrapped it round her, tucking it under her chin.

"That's to remember me by," he said. "You know this is too good a chance to miss. When would I ever get the opportunity of a couple of months intensive skiing, all expenses paid, again? And in one of the best ski centres in the French Alps!"

Emma nodded. "I know," she said. "You were lucky to get a place on the course. But France is such a long way away."

Dave ran his hand through his hair. "I'll phone," he said. "And write, send postcards, e-mail – fax you even. Promise."

Emma nodded. "Just see what happens if you don't," she said smiling, though she felt more like crying.

"That's better," said Dave. "Anyway, you've got a project this term. You'll be so busy you'll hardly notice I'm gone."

As if! The first two weeks Dave was away she had been totally miserable. Then, in desperation, she threw herself into her project. Things got a bit better after that, but Dave was always there at the back of her mind. Even in the midst of her busy

project. And there was always something –
hearing a record they both loved, watching
the Christmas lights go up all over town –
to remind her of him and how much she
missed him. She immersed herself in the
project even more so that she wouldn't have
time to think, so that she would be too tired
at night to lie awake missing him.

A biting gust of wind howled round the
corner of the refectory, driving the sleet in
front of it. Emma clutched the scarf tighter
round her throat. Jassy stopped suddenly
and Emma, head down, cannoned into her.

"Ouch!" said Emma. "What on earth are
you doing, Jassy?"

Jassy pointed to a poster flapping dismally
in the wind. "Look!" she said. "Commotion is
coming to the town hall tomorrow night."

"So what?" said Emma. "Let's get in out of
this wind."

Jassy shook her head. "So what?" she
said. "Are you living on another planet,
Emma? Commotion is only the hottest band
around, that's all."

Emma gave Jassy a push towards the
steps. "Tell me all about it inside," she
said.

Jasmine Hunt, Jassy for short, looked at

her friend in disbelief as they ran up the steps and into the building.

"They're at number one this week," she said. "They came from nowhere and now everybody is mad about them. But they were already doing this tour. So now all these lucky people get to go and see them."

"Including you," said Emma, shaking the drops of water out of her short fair hair.

Jassy looked mournful. "Not including me," she said. "The concert is a sell-out."

Emma grinned. "Oh, come on, Jassy," she said. "You're bound to find somebody with a ticket to spare."

Jassy shook her head, her long glossy black hair swinging. "No chance," she said. "It's Cinderella time for me."

Emma laughed. "Want to bet?" she said. Then she frowned. "So how come I haven't heard of them?"

Jassy steered her into the queue at the self-service counter and picked up a tray.

"You've been living in another world for the last month," she said. "I'm surprised you know what day it is."

Emma pursed her mouth. "Of course I know what day it is. It's the fourteenth," she said.

Jassy selected a tuna salad and shook her head. "Wrong," she said. "It's the fifteenth."

Emma looked at her in horror. "It can't be," she said.

"It is," said Jassy. Then she frowned. "What's the matter? What's so terrible about it being the fifteenth?"

Emma plonked a plate of lasagne down on her tray. "Because Dave comes back on the fifteenth," she said.

"And you forgot!" said Jassy disbelievingly.

"I didn't forget. I just got the date wrong," said Emma defensively.

They shuffled along the queue and paid at the cash desk.

"There's a table," Jassy said and grabbed it before anybody else could.

"How could you get it wrong?" she said, shrugging off her jacket and settling into her chair. "When Dave went off to France you were devastated. You cried every day for a week. You were counting the days you would be apart. I thought you were desperate for the Christmas holidays."

Emma pushed her lasagne around her plate and looked at Jassy.

"Of course I'm dying to see him," she said.

338

"It's just that I promised the kids I would finish the backdrop tonight. I've been so caught up in the production I just forgot everything else."

Jassy shook her head. "The world is passing you by, Emma," she said. "You've done other theatre productions without taking leave of absence from planet earth. What's so special about this production?"

Emma's face lit up. "Oh, it's the kids," she said. "You've no idea how enthusiastic they are. I mean, it's so difficult for them to do even the simplest things. But to put on a pantomime. Well, it's just amazing."

Jassy grinned. "That's not what you said right at the start," she said.

"I was terrified at the start," Emma said. "I didn't realize that just because they're disabled doesn't mean they can't rise to a challenge." She smiled. "Mrs Harper, the headmistress, has had challenge medals made – one for every child."

Jassy raised her eyebrows. "Do you get one too? It's a challenge for you as well, isn't it?" she said.

Emma nodded. "The biggest challenge I've ever had," she replied. "If this show comes off the school will get so much publicity.

They're really in need of equipment and stuff."

"Speaking about publicity," Jassy said. "Did you get Barry Symon?"

Emma flushed with pleasure and nodded. "He agreed," she said. "The kids are beside themselves with excitement."

Jassy looked delighted. Barry Symon was captain of United, the town football team, and to say he was a local hero was understating the matter by a long way.

"I reckon I might come along to the show," she said. "Barry Symon is quite a dish."

Emma laughed. "You don't stand a chance," she said. "The girls at Harlequin School think he's gorgeous and the boys think he's the greatest footballer on two legs. You've got too much competition this time, Jassy. You wouldn't be able to get near him."

Jassy made a face at her. "And I suppose it's just a public relations exercise for you, having him there?" she said.

Emma nodded. "Of course," she said lightly. Then her eyes looked serious. "But really it's all about what these kids can do. Barry Symon was terrific when I asked him to do this. He told me he was laid up with a badly broken leg when he was a kid — multiple fracture. He said he thought then he'd never realize his ambition to be a professional footballer. But he worked and worked at it and eventually he was as good as ever."

"Wow!" said Jassy, impressed. "What a story!"

Emma cupped her chin in her hands. "It's amazing, you know," she said. "These kids can't run and jump and play football, but they get such a buzz out of watching their team, and especially their team captain."

"Barry Symon," said Jassy. "They aren't the only ones that get a buzz out of watching him. But I don't suppose he'd do this for just anybody."

Emma shook her head. "That's what's so great about it," she said. "I mean, the pantomime is a terrific challenge for them but this makes it a really special occasion. This makes the kids feel really important."

"So I hope you've invited plenty of bigwigs," said Jassy.

Emma grinned. "You'd better believe it," she said. "I've invited loads of business people to the show. Once they see the potential these kids have, the equipment will come flooding in." She smiled. "Barry promised to talk to them about sponsorship as well. There are courses and holidays and stuff the kids could go on if the school had the money."

"So it isn't just the production," said Jassy.

Emma shook her head. "It was at first," she said. "But it's much more than that now." She looked at her friend, flushing slightly. "There's a post-graduate course in theatre and special needs. I'm thinking of trying to get on to it when I've finished this course. You know, Jassy, I reckon this is the kind of work I want to do."

Jassy sighed. "What you're doing is so worthwhile," she said. "It makes my design course seem really shallow."

Emma grinned back. "Rubbish!" she said. "And besides, where would my kids be without your pickaxes and shovels?"

Jassy laughed. "I knew I was good for something," she said. "Jasmine Hunt. Pick-axe provider extraordinaire!"

Emma looked across the table at her friend. They had known each other for two years now, since their first term at Redwood. Jassy was doing art and design and Emma was doing theatre studies.

When Emma had chosen to help a local school with a Christmas panto for her project she hadn't realized what she was letting herself in for. Literally! Nobody had told her what kind of school it was. Or perhaps it had been mentioned and she hadn't picked up on it. Emma had been thinking so much about Dave she was only hearing half of what people said to her.

When she found out, she had almost not done it at all. She remembered so clearly that first day when she had visited the Harlequin School.

"So you're Emma," Mrs Harper had said.

Emma smiled. "Emma Pollock," she said. "I'm from Redwood College."

Mrs Harper smiled. "Come and meet the children," she said.

And that had been when Emma had nearly disgraced herself.

Mrs Harper opened a door and led Emma into the main hall of the school. All around her, faces turned and looked at Emma. Smiling faces. Interested, happy. But Emma felt the breath catch in her throat as she realized that every single child was disabled in some way.

She felt panic rising in her. She couldn't

cope with this. She wasn't trained for it. Why hadn't anybody warned her? And, most of all, how was she going to get out of it?

She was about to say something when she felt a touch on her hand and looked down. A little boy in a wheelchair, his thin body twisted, was holding out his hand to her.

Emma took his hand in hers and his thin face lit up. "I'm Tommy," he said. "Can I be a bear?"

Emma couldn't speak. She looked at Mrs Harper. Mrs Harper was studying her with wise grey eyes. She didn't say a word. Emma turned back to Tommy.

"A bear?" she said at last.

Tommy nodded. His head seemed too heavy for the frail body. "In the pantomime," he said. "Mrs Harper says you're going to help us do a pantomime."

Emma swallowed hard and looked around at all the expectant faces. Most of the children were in wheelchairs. Some had walking frames and a few were obviously able to walk unaided but with difficulty.

"You can't be a bear if we do *Dick Whittington*," said a little girl with a diamanté Alice band in her hair and a complicated-looking pair of crutches. "There aren't any bears in *Dick Whittington*, are there?" And she looked at Emma for confirmation.

"That's Jenny," said Tommy. "She doesn't like bears. She wants a pantomime with a witch in it."

Emma took a deep breath. "We could have a bear in *Dick Whittington* if we want," she said to Tommy. "And a witch," she added, turning to Jenny. She looked around the faces. "After all, it's our pantomime. We can have what we like."

She had said the right thing. She saw Tommy's face crease into a smile. Jenny's eyes were like saucers.

"A witch," she breathed.

Emma turned to Mrs Harper and looked at her.

"You didn't know that our children are disabled," Mrs Harper said.

Emma shook her head. "Nobody told me," she replied. "All the note said was the Harlequin School. It didn't say anything about it being a special needs school."

Mrs Harper smiled. "It's all right," she said. "You can change your mind about helping us. Nobody will blame you."

Emma looked into the calm grey eyes. "If

it's OK with you," she said, "I'd like to do this. But I've never worked with disabled children before. I might make a mess of it."

Mrs Harper said nothing for a moment. She studied Emma's earnest face. "Oh, I think you'll do," she said. "The children seem to think so too – or at least Tommy does."

Emma looked down. She hadn't realized she was still holding Tommy's hand.

"Tell you what, Tommy," she said. "We *will* have a bear in this pantomime. Even if it *is Dick Whittington*."

"Or *Aladdin*," said a little girl with a walking frame.

"Or *Mother Goose*," said another.

Emma smiled at Mrs Harper. "Thanks," she said. "Thanks for giving me the chance to do this."

So Emma immersed herself in her project. But nothing could stop her thinking about Dave, about the way he would ruffle her hair, the way his eyes crinkled when he smiled. She wore his scarf all the time and when Tommy asked her if she had a sore throat she nearly burst into tears, because there *did* seem to be a kind of permanent lump in her throat from all the tears she was holding back. But when she looked at the kids she felt really guilty. After all, what did she have to complain about compared to them? If anything helped her through her loneliness it was the kids and in the last few days leading up to the show she worked night and day to make sure it would be a success. They deserved it! She worked so hard she lost track of time. Which was why she had got the date wrong and would have forgotten to go to meet Dave tonight if Jassy hadn't reminded her what day it was.

"Hey, snap out of it," said Jassy now. "Where were you? You've hardly touched your lasagne."

"Sorry," Emma said. "I was miles away. I was just thinking about how I got involved with the Harlequin School."

"Do you still want me to bring those props over tonight?" said Jassy.

Jassy had been a gem, making pickaxes and shovels for Emma. The kids had decided to do *Snow White*, mainly because they all loved the Hi-Ho song. Jenny, the little girl with the Alice band, wanted to be the wicked stepmother and do the "mirror, mirror on the wall" bit. She reckoned that was even better than a witch with a broomstick.

Emma nodded. "Yes, please," she said. "I'll need them for the dress rehearsal tomorrow afternoon."

"Right," said Jassy. "I'll drop them off around eight. What time does Dave arrive?"

Emma dug out her diary and flicked through the pages.

"Nine-fifteen," she said.

"Don't forget to go and meet him," said Jassy.

"As if I would!" she said. Emma gave her a look. "As if I would!"

"Sorry I'm late," Jassy said as she shouldered her way into the Harlequin School hall, carrying a huge cardboard box.

Emma looked up. She was alone in the school hall, finishing painting the backdrop for the scene in the cave – the scene with the bear. Tommy had really thrown himself into the part. Emma had written him a terrific scene where he woke up from his winter sleep and got to frighten the life out of the dwarves while they were digging for gold. He had nearly made himself hoarse already, practising his roaring.

"You aren't that late, are you?" Emma said to Jassy.

Jassy grinned and shook her head. "Time flies when you're having fun," she said. "What are you doing here, anyway? I thought I might have missed you. It's nearly nine o'clock."

Emma smiled back at her friend, then her eyes opened wide. "Oh, no!" she said.

"What?" said Jassy.

"Dave," Emma said. "He gets in at nine-fifteen."

"Well, what did you think I was talking about?" said Jassy. "Honestly, Emma, you'd think I was the one going out with him, not you."

Emma flushed. There had been a time when she thought Jassy really liked Dave – and not just as a friend.

"I'll get there in time," she said, throwing down her paintbrush and rushing for her jacket. "Is it raining?"

"Hail!" said Jassy with a grimace. "Just the sort of weather for hanging around draughty bus stations. Dave will be thrilled."

"I'm going, I'm going," yelled Emma, grabbing her scarf and her bag. "I'll be back to clear this stuff up." She hesitated. "What about this backdrop?" she said. "I have to get it done tonight. The show is tomorrow night."

Jassy shook her head. "Go!" she said. "I'll carry on with it."

Emma went.

The hail was turning to snow as she ran down the street. The bus station was at the other end of town. She would never make it in time and she already had a stitch in her side. Her hair hung in rats' tails, dripping on to her face.

I must look terrible, she thought as the lights of the bus station came into view.

Flakes of snow whirled in the light as she rushed through the entrance and searched wildly around. Then she caught sight of him and her heart thudded. It was so odd. She had been so caught up in her project she hadn't given much thought to what she would say to him when she saw him again. It was funny to see him now, before he saw her. So familiar but strange because she hadn't seen him for two months.

He was standing in the middle of the concourse, rucksack over one broad shoulder, looking at his watch, checking it with the clock above the booking office. She looked at the dark hair that curled slightly at the nape of his neck, at the tilt of his head. He was deeply tanned, his skin glowing against the darkness of his hair. He looked absurdly out of place in the drab, grimy bus station. Although she couldn't see his face, she knew exactly what his expression would be. Anxious and more than a bit annoyed.

She felt nervous suddenly and shy. *This is ridiculous*, she told herself. *It's Dave. How can you feel shy?*

Then he turned and saw her and his face split into a smile. He tossed his rucksack to the ground and strode towards her and she ran to him, folding herself into his arms, holding her face up for his kiss. Then she didn't feel shy any longer. It was Dave, her Dave. And he was just the same.

"Where have you been?" he said at last and she smiled up at him.

"Let's go and I'll show you," she said, tucking her arm into his.

"Go where?" said Dave.

Emma smiled. "It's my project," she said. "I have to go back and clear a few things up."

"The first night I get back?" said Dave. "You've got to work?"

Emma looked at him, puzzled. "It doesn't seem like work," she said. "I don't mind."

Dave's eyes were dark as he looked at her. "But maybe I do," he said.

For a moment Emma was taken aback. Then she reached up and kissed him lightly. "Don't be grumpy," she said. "It's all in a good cause."

But, as she told him about Tommy and his bear scene and Barry Symon coming to present the challenge medals, she didn't see his eyes darken and his mouth tighten.

All he said was, "I've had a really grim journey. The heating on the train in France broke down, the ferry crossing was really rough and I've been sitting on that bus for hours. I was looking forward to some time together – just the two of us."

But by that time they had reached the school and Emma pushed open the door. "You can give me a hand then we'll go for a pizza, how's that?"

Dave's mouth twisted. "Great," he said. "Just great!"

"Dave!" Jassy yelled, flying across the room to meet him. "How are you? You look terrific! Was the journey lousy?"

Dave unhitched his rucksack and gave

Jassy a bear hug, swinging her round in his arms. "Great to see you!" he said smiling down at her.

Emma relaxed. Dave looked much more like himself now, chatting away to Jassy as she gathered up her materials and put the finishing touches to the backdrop.

Dave and Jassy helped her put up the scenery and she dusted off her hands.

"That's me finished," she said.

Dave looked at his watch. "And it's only half past ten," he said.

Emma bit her lip. "Already? Oh, Dave, I'm sorry. But we can still catch the pizza house."

For a moment she thought he was going to say something else. Then he ruffled her hair and smiled. "You always could twist me round your finger," he said. "Come on. I've got a surprise for you. I'll tell you about it over a deep pan pepperoni with olives and extra cheese."

"What surprise?" said Emma excitedly. "Tell me now!"

Dave reached into his inside pocket and pulled out a couple of tickets. "The best seats in the house for Commotion," he said.

Jassy squeaked. "Where did you get

those?" she said. "They're like gold. I'd give anything to be able to go."

Dave grinned. "I had to pay over the odds for them from a guy I met on the bus," he said. "But I reckoned an early Christmas present might go down well," and he looked at Emma.

Emma looked blankly back at him. "You mean the concert in the Town Hall?" she said. "Tomorrow night?"

Dave nodded. "Can't believe it, can you?" he said.

Emma shook her head. "It isn't that," she said. "I can't go."

Dave's face fell. "Can't go?" he said.

"Tomorrow night is the kids' pantomime," said Emma. "I can't miss it. It's my project. I've put a lot into it. And besides, I don't want to miss it for a pop concert."

Dave's mouth tightened and he looked at her. "You know, ever since I got off that bus and you met me – late," he said, "all you've done is talk about this project. Is that all you can think about?"

Emma felt herself going pale. "It's important to me," she said.

"More important than I am?" said Dave. "What about all that stuff you were giving me before I went away? I was the one that wasn't to forget you. It seems to me you're the one that's been doing the forgetting."

"It isn't like that," said Emma.

But Dave was still looking at her, his mouth grim. "Oh no?" he said. "It looks like that to me. I'm beginning to think I'm not important to you."

"That isn't true," Emma protested.

Dave ran a hand through his hair. Emma noticed for the first time how tired he looked. Underneath his tan his face was pale and strained. He looked exhausted. She remembered that he had been travelling all day and that the skiing course in France, for all that it sounded like a holiday, would have been a lot of hard work.

"Look, Emma," he said. "I haven't seen you for more than two months. I've tried phoning you but you were always out at this project of yours. But that was OK. I mean, you've got your work to do and I was the one that went away on the course. But I thought that when I got back I'd get some kind of welcome. Instead of that I seem to be in the way, don't I?"

"No!" Emma said, her voice a mere whisper.

"So how come I find you're too busy to

spend time with me?" said Dave.

"I'm not," said Emma. "It's just that..." Her voice trailed off.

"Just that what?" Dave said. "I wish you'd said you were going to be tied up. Then I might have stayed on in France for a few days like the others did. I might have taken the chance of getting in some more skiing. And I wouldn't have got these tickets."

Emma swallowed hard. She had never seen Dave like this before.

"So, I suggest you make up your mind," he said. "Either you come to the concert with me or you don't. If you don't, I'll know what to think. And you don't have to worry about me. I can always get somebody else to go to the concert. So, the ball's in your court, Emma. Call me if you change your mind."

For a moment he looked at her and she saw the hurt in his eyes. Then he was striding towards the door, picking up his rucksack.

"Dave!" Emma called. "That's just not fair!"

He turned in the doorway. "Fair?" he said. "Who said anything about fair? It's the way I feel, Emma."

Jassy stood by the door, a worried frown on her face.

Dave looked down at her and smiled ruefully. "Sorry to drag you into this, Jassy," he said and kissed her lightly on the cheek.

She looked up at him, concern in her eyes.

"See you!" he said softly to her and then he was gone.

Emma looked at Jassy and felt a pit where her heart should have been. Her eyes blurred with tears.

"He wouldn't even listen," she said as the tears ran scalding down her cheeks. "He didn't want to know."

Jassy sighed. "Watch out, Emma," she said gently, putting her arm round her friend's shoulders. "You can't just fob him off like that. You'll lose him if you aren't careful."

Emma shoved her hair back out of her streaming eyes. "He didn't mean it," she said, searching her pockets for a hankie. "He was just tired because of the journey and annoyed because I was late."

"And what about all those phone calls?" said Jassy, handing her a tissue. "Did you return them?"

Emma bit her lip. "I was so busy," she said.

"Then he was right," said Jassy. "You were too busy to be bothered with him."

"But it wasn't like that," said Emma. "Have you any idea how much work these kids have put in?"

"Has Dave?" said Jassy.

"What do you mean?" Emma said, mopping her cheeks.

Jassy shook her head in despair. "Have you ever really talked to Dave about this project? Tried to involve him? Tried to make him understand how important it is to you?"

"How could I involve him? He was miles away!" Emma said. "And, anyway, I talked to him about it tonight. I talked about nothing else."

Jassy didn't say a word.

"You think he feels left out, don't you?" Emma said.

"Don't *you*?" said Jassy.

Emma tossed her hair and scrubbed at her cheeks. "This isn't Dave's sort of thing," she said. "He's only interested in sport and stuff. And anyway after tomorrow night it'll all be over."

"It might," said Jassy.

Emma turned on her accusingly. "What do you mean?"

Jassy spread out her hands. "You heard

him," she said. "Don't blame me if he gets fed up waiting for you to have time for him. All I'm doing is trying to warn you."

Emma looked at her friend, at her long silky black hair and her big dark eyes. Dave had kissed her – on the cheek. But still, it was a kiss.

Why was Jassy so eager to warn her? What exactly was she warning her about?

"Are you coming?" Jassy said.

Emma shook her head and stuffed the crumpled, sodden hankie in her pocket.

"I've still got a couple of things to do," she said. "You go."

Jassy opened her mouth as if to say something. Then she changed her mind.

"OK," she said. "See you!"

"See you!" Emma replied.

Dave had said that to Jassy. But it was just a phrase, wasn't it? It didn't mean anything. Emma took a deep breath. She had work to do. She would phone Dave tomorrow.

Backstage the excitement was tangible.

"How do I look?" Jenny said.

Emma looked at the little girl's face. She was fizzing with excitement. You could see

359

that her cheeks were flushed even through the greenish tinge of her make-up.

"Aaaargh!" said Emma, pretending to be scared to death. "You look gruesome."

"Good!" said Jenny in a satisfied voice. "I've got to frighten the life out of those dwarves, you know."

"You and Tommy both," said Emma. "I tell you, it's the dwarves I feel sorry for."

Emma looked to where the seven dwarves were lined up, their pointed caps bobbing as they whispered excitedly together in the wings.

One of them looked round. It looked like Sneezy. "Is he here yet?" he called.

Emma smiled. There was no need to ask who he meant. "Not yet," she said. "He'll be here soon."

"Ten minutes to curtain up," Mrs Harper said behind her. "Let's hope Barry Symon enjoys the performance – if he arrives."

Emma gave her an encouraging smile. "He will – and he will," she said. "It's going to be fine. Don't worry. How is the audience?"

Mrs Harper rolled her eyes. "Almost as excited as the kids," she said. "All their brothers and sisters have brought auto-graph books with them and the local press is out in force."

"Great," said Emma. Then her voice tailed off as she looked beyond Mrs Harper to the other side of the stage.

"Excuse me, Mrs Harper," she said. "I'll be back in a minute."

Somewhere a telephone was ringing but Emma barely heard it. All she was conscious of was Dave, standing in the wings on the other side of the stage, looking at her.

She walked towards him slowly across the stage. Behind the curtain she could hear the audience shuffling and chattering. But the sounds seemed to come from a long way off. Her whole concentration was on Dave. He hadn't been in touch since last night. And she had been so busy all day she hadn't had time to get in touch with him – at least that's what she had told herself.

Now, all she wanted was for him to say everything was fine, missing the pop concert didn't matter. But he just stood there looking at her as she walked towards him across the set.

When she reached him, he didn't even touch her. "I'm *really* sorry I can't go to the concert, Dave," she said.

He looked deep into her eyes, his own eyes dark and unreadable. Around them children chattered and squealed, bumping their wheelchairs together, adjusting their costumes.

"Can you fix my head?" said Tommy from his wheelchair.

Emma bent automatically to fasten the ties at the back of Tommy's furry bear mask. The mask was a bit amateurish looking but Tommy didn't mind. He had helped to make it. In fact all the costumes looked a bit lopsided. But Emma was a firm believer in the kids doing as much of the work as they could – even if it didn't look totally professional. Jassy had been terrific helping with the stuff they couldn't manage but anything they could make themselves, they had made. With a bit of glitter and a lot of pizzazz, it would look fine from where the audience was sitting.

But now, when she looked around with Dave standing there, she wondered what it looked like to an outsider. To her it was so important. To the kids it was more exciting than Christmas. But what would an outsider think? Would they see it just as a half-baked amateur production with a lot of kids who weren't too sure of their lines or their moves? She caught herself up. An outsider? Was that how she saw Dave?

"What's wrong?" said Tommy. "What are you looking so miserable about?"

Emma looked at him. All she could see of him was a pair of big brown eyes peering through the eye holes in his bear head mask. But that was enough to see the concern he felt.

"Nothing's the matter," she said. "Everything is just fine."

She saw Tommy's thin little body relax.

"Oh, that's good," he said. "For a minute I thought something terrible had happened — like Barry Symon not coming."

Emma smiled. "Nothing is going to go wrong. I promise."

Tommy looked up at her and the brown eyes behind the mask sparkled. "That's all right then," he said. "If you promise."

And he turned his wheelchair to position himself for his entrance.

When Emma looked up, Dave was watching her very carefully.

"Is this what you've been spending all your time on?" he said and his voice sounded harsh in her ears.

Her head came up and she looked at him and spoke very clearly.

"Yes," she said. "It might not be perfect, but it's the best we can do and it's important to me."

"Phone for you, Emma," said a voice behind her and Mrs Harper was standing there, a mobile phone in her hand.

Emma took the phone.

"Emma Pollock here," she said as Mrs Harper went off to get the squirrels and rabbits lined up ready to come on. Somebody switched on the tape player and the introductory music filled the hall. The curtain began to swing back, creaking as it went. At the back of her mind Emma hoped it wouldn't stick the way it had done at the dress rehearsal that afternoon.

Then she realized who was on the phone. She listened as the voice at the other end spoke in her ear.

"What?" she said, her face draining of colour. "Are you sure you can't make it?"

The voice spoke again and Emma nodded. She watched as Tommy wheeled himself onstage to a burst of applause.

Then the rabbits and squirrels and dwarves and elves trundled and bumped and lurched their way on to the stage singing the Hi-Ho song. The audience went wild.

"No, no," she whispered into the phone. "Of course I understand. Thanks for ringing."

"What is it?" said Dave.

Emma turned to him. "That was Barry Symon," she said. "He can't make it. There's a training session tonight for the big game tomorrow and they've all got orders to be there. No excuses, no exceptions, he says."

"You mean you've lost your special guest?" said Dave.

Emma shook her head. "He was more than that," she said. "The kids wrote a special bit for the end of the panto just for him. They're going to be so disappointed. And he was going to give out the challenge medals."

"But how could he do this?" said Dave.

Emma shrugged. "It isn't his fault. He can't cut training," she said. "It was a last minute thing. The manager is really nervous about tomorrow's game."

Dave didn't say anything.

Emma brushed a tear away. She hadn't realized she was crying.

"So it's all been for nothing," she said. "No Barry Symon, no publicity. No publicity, no sponsors. No sponsors, no equipment, no courses, no trips. I suppose you think I've wasted my time."

"Do *you*?" Dave said. "I thought this was really important to you – just putting on the show. Just the fact that these kids could do it."

Emma shrugged. "It is," she said shortly. She looked at her watch. "You'd better go. The pop concert will be starting soon."

He was silent for a moment. Then he said, "You could still come with me."

Emma drew in her breath sharply. "And run away?" she said. She shook her head. "No. I've got to tell them Barry isn't coming." She looked towards the stage where the kids were singing their hearts out – with actions. "But not till the very last minute," she said. "I'll tell them at the end, just before he's due to go on. At least they can enjoy the rest of the pantomime that way."

Dave nodded, his lids half lowered so that she couldn't see his eyes.

"I'd better go then," he said.

"Yes," said Emma.

He turned away, then turned back. "You

haven't got Jassy's phone number, have you?"

Emma felt the breath stop in her throat. Then she recovered herself and gave him the number automatically.

He looked at her for a moment, then turned away.

"Thanks," he said as he went.

She watched him go, his long stride taking him out of the wings, down the steps into the auditorium, out of the hall, out of her life.

"Ready with the curtain?" Mrs Harper said behind her. Emma cast a quick look round. Mrs Harper, head down, was getting the papier mâché cave ready to shove on-stage. She looked past Emma, towards the stage.

"Here they come," she said.

Emma dashed the tears from her eyes and took a deep breath as kids trundled off the stage, eyes shining, the applause thunderous behind them. Her life was in ruins. She had lost Dave and the kids' big treat was going to turn into a terrible disappointment. What had she promised Tommy? That nothing would go wrong. What a joke! She could imagine only too well the expressions on those shining faces when she told them their hero hadn't come. But the show must go on. Isn't that what they always said?

"Ready!" she said and hauled grimly on the curtain cord.

The roar of the applause went on for ages. The kids were brought on-stage for encore after encore until Mrs Harper, smiling determinedly, brought the show to an end and introduced Emma.

Emma looked around the shining, expectant faces gathered round her on the stage. Then she looked down into the audience. Parents, teachers, sisters, brothers, aunts, uncles, grans and grandads all sat there waiting for the big moment when Barry Symon would come on stage and hand out the challenge badges. Every child would have a badge. Every child would have a photograph to take home and hang in a place of honour.

Emma cleared her throat. Mrs Harper had offered to do the announcement for her but Emma had insisted. It had been her idea to ask Barry Symon in the first place. She had got the kids all worked up. She would have to be the one to let them down.

"Ladies and gentlemen and children," she said. Then her voice dried up.

"He's coming now, isn't he?" piped Tommy from his wheelchair.

Emma looked down at him and shook her head.

"Oh, Tommy," she said.

But Tommy wasn't looking at her. Instead he was looking at the back of the hall where someone was pushing the double doors wide.

Emma looked up. Dave was swinging the doors back to the walls and behind him, dressed in full kit, came Barry Symon. And behind him came the whole of the United team.

Emma felt her jaw drop open as she watched the players stride up the aisle to roars of applause and cheering. They were waving to the fans, shaking hands, having a word here and there and even stopping off to give autographs. Then they were leaping up on to the stage, in amongst the kids, talking, laughing, joking with them. Mrs Harper brought the badges out, clearly bewildered.

Players started pinning badges on, cameras flashed and Emma saw a man in a suit run up the stairs on to the stage.

"That's the manager," said a voice behind her. "Be nice to him. He's not such a bad guy after all."

Emma turned to find Dave smiling down at her. She opened her mouth but no sound came out.

"Look!" said Dave.

Emma watched as the manager dug into a carrier bag and drew out jersey after jersey, draping the brightly coloured garments around the kids. The kids whooped with delight. The audience roared its approval, Mrs Harper was in tears. It was pandemonium.

"What's going on?" said Emma to Dave at last.

Dave took her in his arms.

"You wanted a footballer," he said. "I got you a team! Happy Christmas!"

"But how?" said Emma.

Dave grinned. "I just marched round to the football ground, bluffed my way in and told them what they were missing. Once I'd finished you couldn't hold them back."

"But what did you tell them?" said Emma. "How did you get them here? What about the training session?"

Dave looked at the stage. Tommy's face

was ablaze with happiness as Barry Symon tried on his bear head. Jenny's hair was standing on end and her green make-up was beginning to run but she looked incredibly proud as the manager of United admired her challenge badge.

"How did you do it?" said Emma again.

"I told them what I saw here," Dave said. "I told them about Tommy and Jenny and Mrs Harper and I told them about you."

Emma's breath was a bit ragged.

"But why?" she said. "I thought you'd gone to the concert with Jassy."

He looked puzzled. "Jassy?" he said. "Oh, I gave her a ring and left the tickets at the Town Hall box office for her. I hope she found somebody to go with."

Emma was still shaken.

"But why?" she said again.

"You said this was important to you," he said. "But you didn't tell me this was what it was like. Until tonight I didn't understand."

Emma shook her head. "I closed you out," she said. "I was so busy."

Dave looked down at her. "There's no need to close me out," he said. "There are some specialist sports courses I'd like to do, you know. Now that I've seen what you've been doing, I'd like to try working with kids like these as well. Don't ever leave me out in the cold again, Emma."

It was a moment before Emma could speak. "I didn't think you'd be interested," she said.

Dave's eyes darkened. "In you?" he said. "I'm interested in everything you do. I always will be." He smiled. "Is it always going to be like this for you?"

Emma nodded. "I think so. Do you mind?"

Dave looked serious. "I did when I felt left out," he said. "But I realize now what I love about you. I couldn't love you so much if you didn't care about these kids as much as you do."

Emma let out a shaky sigh of relief. "That's good," she said. "Because I'm pretty sure I know now what I want to do with my life."

Dave smiled. "I hope it includes me."

Emma reached out a hand and touched his cheek.

"Oh, it does," she said. "It most certainly does."

The cheers rose to a deafening crescendo on the stage as the players posed for photos

372

with the kids and the whole audience erupted in United's song.

"Want to join in?" said Dave.

Emma drew his head down towards her.

"Later," she said. "First things first."

And, as he kissed her, she forgot all about footballers and pantomimes and even little Tommy. There were some things in life you just had to concentrate on one hundred per cent.

P✹INT CRiME

If you like Point Horror, you'll love Point Crime!

A murder has been committed ... Whodunnit? Was it
the arch rival, the mystery stranger or the best friend?
An exciting series of crime novels, with tortuous plots
and lots of suspects, designed to keep the reader
guessing till the very last page.